PRAISE FOR NAOMI NASH
AND *YOU ARE SO CURSED!*

"How can you go wrong with a book about a faux witch, a hot guy, a poop-crazy goat and those girls you just love to hate? . . . This book finds a hilarious medium. Definitely recommended for the confused person in all of us."

—*RT BOOKclub*

OH, WHAT A TANGLED WEB . . .

Without warning, I was blinded by light. Someone's flashlight burned holes in my retinas. For a panicked second I thought I was going to lose my grip on my ladder. I clutched the rope until its spiky fibers made my eyes water. "Chloe?" someone said above me. "Don't move."

Something about the voice I recognized. "Connor?" I asked, pulling myself up another rung.

"Don't . . . seriously, don't . . ."

I felt his hand grab my upper arm as I clawed for the surface. "What are you doing?" I was utterly surprised when he started to haul me up with such force that I knew I'd have enormous hand-shaped bruises on the undersides of my biceps tomorrow. He wasn't graceful about it, either. Next thing I knew, we were a tangle of arms and legs and torsos on the side of the shaft's opening. "What is the BFD?" I asked him, seriously annoyed at his intervention.

He didn't have to say a word. He just aimed the beam of his flashlight at the floor stakes supporting the ladder.

One of them was intact and perfectly fine. The other one was missing.

Who had cut it?

Other SMOOCH books by Naomi Nash:
YOU ARE *SO* CURSED!

CHLOE,
QUEEN OF DENIAL

NAOMI NASH

SMOOCH NEW YORK CITY

This book is dedicated to Chloe and Sophia Johnson—
live your lives as bravely as you can!

SMOOCH ®

July 2004

Published by

Dorchester Publishing Co., Inc.
200 Madison Avenue
New York, NY 10016

ISBN 0-8439-5377-2

The name "SMOOCH" and its logo are trademarks of Dorchester Publishing Co., Inc.

Printed in the United States of America.

Visit us on the web at www.smoochya.com.

ACKNOWLEDGMENTS

I owe a thousand thanks to Patty Woodwell for catching the thousand errors my own eyes couldn't; to Andrew Wright for designing the frightening logo for the Dig Egypt! program; to Craig Symons for returning all my overdue library books after I finished; to Kate Seaver for suggesting the project; and to Michelle Grajkoswki for just being fabulous. I couldn't have had a better collaborator in this scheme than Katie Maxwell, who is an absolute blast to work with, particularly when she's yelling at her hounds.

CHLOE,
QUEEN OF DENIAL

One

Across barren sands an oasis waited for me, green and cool and shimmering with water. Sunlight made the dunes painfully bright, but my slitted lids held no moisture. Only two miles to go, and I could drink long and deep. "Water!" I croaked, but no one was there to hear me.

Then I heard a voice whispering my name. "Chloe."

Hold on. Was I hallucinating? Or was I already dead? I'd been told that people lost in the desert sometimes heard things . . . right before they went totally insane. I shook my head, hoping the motion might jar out the voice. Where had it come from? Behind me was only my shuffled trail in the sand, which even now was being erased by desert winds hotter than the ground underfoot. Ahead of me was nothing but wasteland. And above, Egypt's white-hot sun, blazing down as if it wanted to burn from the landscape any trace of me it could find. *You're going to die here,* I told myself. *You should never have stepped foot in this most ancient of lands. You're a fake.*

I shook my head again. No. I had absolutely no intention of dying here. I had not come all the way from Seattle to collapse in the wilderness, my corpse picked over by buzzards, with no grave other than the shifting sands. The oasis was only two miles away, and there I could quench my thirst with water, sweet water. . . .

"Chloe." I heard the voice again. "Chloe! Wake up!"

For, like, a split second after I opened my eyes, I was convinced my friends had rescued me from certain death in the middle of Egypt's endless sands. But no. I seemed to be in a dark space, lying on a cot that had transformed my butt into a lumpy sack of potatoes. I hadn't been saved at all. I had been sleeping. When I licked my cracked lips, I realized how thirsty I was. No wonder my dreams were of the desert.

No. Wait. The past week came flooding back to me. I *was* in the desert. In Egypt. The Valley of the Servitors, working on the tomb of Tekhen and Tekhnet, to be precise.

The four-letter word that came flying out of my mouth was one everybody in my family had used at some time or another, but it wasn't one I usually said louder than a whisper. My tentmate, Sue Chatterjee, must have heard it, though, because her face suddenly appeared over the tips of my toes. "I know!" she said.

Huh? That didn't make sense. And what was she doing down there?

"But Chloe . . . don't move, okay? It'll be all right." Sue's brown eyes stretched wide with fear and concern. She had a habit of gnawing on the tip of her big, dark braid whenever she was nervous, but now she was practically sucking the color right out of it.

"I'm okay," I said sleepily. What time was it? Was I late for breakfast? "I was only dreaming."

When I tried to sit up in my cot, Sue pointed at my stomach and screamed loudly enough to shatter glass, "Don't move!"

I froze and scrunched up my face. Okay, who substituted crazy powder for her Tang this morning? There was nothing on me except for a little woven bracelet someone had left there. It was kind of pretty, all stripes of black and greenish brown with fringy bits. . . .

To my horror, the bracelet lifted its fringy bits and began to crawl in my direction. That was no jewelry. A scorpion was slowly making its way across my blanket! When suddenly I sucked in a lungful of air, the scorpion stopped, quivering its tail as if it were about to strike.

Don't move? The *heck!* Somehow I think—and I bet about 99 percent of the world population would agree with me on this—that when a girl wakes up and sees a scorpion perched on her belly, moving is the first thing she wants to do! I peered at Sue over my blanket's edge, my heart pounding so furiously that it seemed to be flopping around the inside of my mouth. For the first time I noticed the other Dig Egypt! kids crowded outside around the tent flap, all of them watching me. None of them was doing a thing. Oh, no, that would be too helpful. They all merely stood there, looking at me as if I were dead already.

Over my racing pulse, my brain registered how annoyed I was at that.

Three nights ago, right after our arrival at the camp, the archaeologist in charge of excavation had presented a long lecture on desert-survival tactics. Between her warnings on snakes, insects, disease, rabid dogs, and emergency terrorist evacuation procedures, she'd so badly scared the six of us on the excavation team that we all wished we still wore diapers.

Desperately my mind chugged away while I tried to remember vital information that was coming back to me only in dribs and drabs. Okay, Dr. Battista had said there were green African scorpions and black African scorpions. One of them was bad news, the other not so much. But which was which? Black for bad? Green for poison? This was important stuff here, so why wasn't I remembering anything she'd said?

Oh, yeah. Maybe because the adults in charge decided to give us all that lifesaving information immediately after I'd spent twenty-one hours on airplanes from Seattle to New York to Paris to Cairo, followed by a bumpy drive in vans from Cairo to Luxor, so that I'd felt like a zombie extra from *Night of the Living Dead,* that's why.

Smart, folks. Real smart. I cursed whoever it was who'd had *that* bright idea.

Meanwhile, the scorpion certainly wasn't hailing a taxi and toddling off for a night at the opera. On pointed claws it marched up the blanket, readying its tail to strike after every one of my shudders. I was going to die, right here and now, just like in my dream. The only way I would get home from Egypt would be in a body bag. Thanks bunches, Mom and Dad!

No. Nuh-uh. Not this time. I absolutely refused to die unshowered and in my sleepwear. "Sue," I said in a soft voice that sounded much calmer than I felt. "Sunita!" I snapped, using her full name. Sue seemed more concerned with calming Deidre Pierce—the camp coward, who whimpered and sobbed while the arachnid tried to find the ideal spot to impale me—than with my immediate demise. Now, how could I remember that scorpions were arachnids and not insects, but I couldn't figure out whether I was about to require an airlift to a hospital or just an ice pack and some aspirin? Life was just *so* unfair sometimes.

"Sorry," said my tentmate. "Deidre's pretty scared."

"*Deidre's* scared!" The heck! "Clear the others away. I'm

4

going to do something." I bet neither kid on the restoration team, both snug in their real beds in a converted monastery house miles away, had to deal with this kind of crap.

"I got a shout out for Dag," I heard Bo call from outside. "Just keep cool."

"Ms. Sorensson is coming," Sue echoed. "She'll know what to do." Then, to the girl at her other side with the short-bobbed dark hair, she added, "*Le*, um, how do you say, *est arrivant*. What's 'chaperone' in French?"

Oh, fine. I was about to meet my maker while Sue translated my plight to our Parisian student. " 'Chaperone' *is* French, Sunita!" I yelled at her.

I was sunk. Our flaky chaperone would take one look at the scorpion and run in the opposite direction. On second thought, the scorpion might take a look at Dagmar Sorensson and scamper away, scared for its life. Still, it wasn't a chance I wanted to take. "I'm not waiting for that redheaded clown," I barked back. Immediately I noticed how strained and strange my voice sounded. Could they hear it too?

"Please please please please please don't do anything, Chloe." For the first time in my life, I actually saw someone bite her lip and wring her hands. The only thing keeping Sunita from being the overacting heroine of a silent movie was a big old villain with a waxed mustache tying her to railroad tracks. "That scorpion could kill you! *La mort*," she added for Mallorie Dupuis.

The French girl gasped. *"La mort!"*

All rightie, then. That settled that! Black must be the bad kind.

"Okay," I said aloud. "You . . . just . . . stay . . . calm." I didn't know whether I was talking to myself or to the scorpion. Maybe a little of both. "I'm going to . . . That's it." I slid my hands from under the covers to the top of the blanket until the scorpion suddenly paused. Did they have noses? I didn't think so. Still, it looked as if it was sniffing in my direction. "That's right," I told it, swallowing heavily. "Be still."

Thank goodness I had tucked in the bottom of my blanket the night before—in case some bug or mouse or snake had decided to crawl up under it, in fact. Fat lot of good that had done to keep deadly bugs—*arachnids,* whatever—from setting up shop on my vital regions. My foresight had given me a perfect anchor for the blanket, though. I began to lift the rough covering up and away from my body.

Outside the tent, Deidre Pierce shrieked as simultaneously the scorpion suddenly dashed two inches in the direction of my face. Annoying, that. "Too fast," I told myself, slowing down my movements. "It's okay, little scorpion." I kept my voice down to a whisper, aware that everything was so quiet around me now that I could hear the chatter of the cooks and the sound of clashing dishes from the mess tent, halfway across the camp. "It's okay." With some extremely gradual lifting, I managed to raise the blanket a good three or four inches from my body. The scorpion stayed very, very still.

While I eyed the creepy-crawly, I pulled myself up to a sitting position, holding the blanket as motionless as possible. There was a tense moment when it began to pull away from one of the corners, but within a few seconds I was able to swing my feet over the cot's edge. No mean feat, considering how trembly my legs felt.

"Okay." I used my singsong voice, very softly. "Is everyone away from the flap? Because I'm going to get rid of this very nice . . . sweet . . . good scorpion." By now I'd managed to ease myself to my feet, the top edge of the blanket still in my hands. The only way the thing could hurt me now was if it jumped at my face. They couldn't do that, could they? Could they jump? Only Mexican beans jumped, right? Maybe I didn't want to know.

I heard noises from the other kids when I shifted myself around so that I faced the bed, but all my attention was focused on the deadly little bundle of sharp pointy bits and venom circling the middle of the cot. With my left hand I tugged the far end of the blanket from the bottom of the bed frame until it was completely loose. "Okay," I said, ignoring the slight shake in my voice. The kids would panic if I didn't make myself sound calm. "Everyone stand clear." I held my breath. This was it.

"Now!"

I grabbed the four corners of the blanket and, holding it as far away from my body as I could, stooped and ran out under the tent flap. My wrist banged against the center tent pole on the way out, and my bundle with it. I didn't stop running, though. Like I was going to open up the blanket before I had to? Hardly. Still, I felt a twinge at the thought that I might have smashed my little passenger. Aquarians like me didn't get along with Scorpios, generally, but I hated crushing bugs. I couldn't even kill a spider. This was kind of the same thing as getting rid of a spider outdoors, right?

As fast as my legs could take me, I ran and ran to the edge of camp, where the slope ended in a sharp drop to the canyon below. Pebbles cut into the soles of my feet, but I didn't care. At any other time I would've grudgingly admired the sight of the ancient catacombs carved into the cliffs below, almost colorful against the sunrise. With a lethal critter in tow, however, let's just say I was not in a rosy early-morning mood. I flung out the blanket over the edge of the cliff as if I were shaking the dust and sand from it. "Buh-bye!" I yelled after the scorpion, expecting my gesture to send it sailing out into the air and over the cliff.

Only nothing flew out.

Oh, crud. I dropped the blanket on the ground. Against its gray weave I saw no trace of scorpion. No scorpion goo from being banged against the tent pole. Nothing. Gingerly I grabbed one of the corners and flung it over. Nothing there, either. But then where . . . ?

"Chloe!" one of the Tousson twins called out in his deep voice from the camp's edge. When I turned, all the Dig Egypt! kids were watching me. For the first time I noticed that most of them still wore the T-shirts and sweats that we all used for nightclothes. Sue must have roused them straight out of their beds. "Behind you!"

I followed the direction of the Tousson twin's finger. I'll be darned if the little fiend wasn't skittering in my direction, hell-bent on plunging its twitchy stinger into the fleshiest part of me it could find. I was so startled by its velocity that my legs instinctively jerked as I yelped and jumped . . .

. . . and side-kicked the scorpion right over the slope edge. I barely felt it brush my toes as it went flying out into the air. It was with amazement that I watched it fall and disappear beyond the rock beneath our feet. Wait a minute! *I* did that?

"Whoa!" said Bo, running forward.

"Mon Dieu!" Mallorie jogged up beside me and looked over the side of the cliff.

I peered over too. *Mon Dieu,* all right. It was goner than gone. Score one for scorpion kickball!

Before I even realized what I'd done, I was surrounded by the other kids. One of the twins—I still had a hard time telling Seth apart from Cyrus—was clapping me on the back. Someone was picking up my blanket and folding it. Several more were congratulating me. In my thudding head I couldn't even distinguish the gabble into words, but I knew I didn't deserve a word of it.

When my eyes cleared and I looked back to camp, I found the path blocked by Kathy Klemper and, looming behind her, Dagmar Sorensson. Dag wore a head of curly red hair cut into an unfortunate wedge I hadn't seen since I stumbled across some of my mom's more painfully embarrassing record albums from the eighties—Dag looked so much like a fast-food clown that we called her "Rona McDonald" behind her back. Well, that's what I called her. It had kind of caught on among the excavation team kids, though.

It was obvious ol' carrottop had been giving some new kid a fifty-cent tour of the archaeologist's camp. He trailed behind her with his suitcase, shoulders slumped, his face hidden beneath his baseball cap.

Even though the rest of us still wore our sleepwear, Kathy was already in her khakis. Her tight ponytail hung down in a perfect tress at the back of her head. Don't ask me how she kept so tidy—after three days of not washing it, my short black hair was a greasy mess of tangles and snarls that I kept concealed with a bandanna most of the day. Kathy's expression was so spiteful that you could have collected it in fancy spray bottles and sold it as Calvin Klein's Utter Disdain. "There she is," she said in one of those voices that could curdle wet concrete. "Did you see, Ms. Sorensson? Chloe *kicked* local fauna over the cliff." I'd known I hated Kathy three hours into the project; three days in and I wished she'd been the one I'd kicked.

Just the month before in tenth-grade English I'd read a

short story about a guy named Dorian Gray who never seemed to grow older, though the painting of himself he'd stuffed in his attic practically collected Social Security checks. I had a private theory that Dag had some kind of similar deal going on with her laundry. Her uniforms never wrinkled or grew dirty, but somewhere in someone's attic was a basket filled with filthy clothes that smelled like rotting corpses with a twist of skunk. I suspected Dag was using more water than her ration. "Chloe Bryce!" she snapped.

I tried not to watch her wedge of orange hair bob atop her head as she stomped over. "How many times I am telling you? Little birds and bees of the desert regions of Egypt are *not* to be made the trampling upon. We are being guests here. We tread with the light foot!" Dagmar's Swedish accent always made me feel as if I were lurching around in a roller coaster.

"My foot *are* the light foot!" I protested ungrammatically. She made it sound like I made a habit of drop-kicking every Egyptian bird, bug, and mammal I saw! "That scorpion trampled on me!"

"If it makes the trampling on you, it is from you disturbing the tomb of the dead," Dagmar proclaimed. For someone who worked at an archaeological site, she had a weird superstitious streak. "It is curse! You will be being dead from bite of scorpion!"

When Kathy Klemper had the nerve to smirk, I muttered with no little bitterness, "Sounds like you'd be happier if I died of a scorpion bite."

"I am hearing nonsense," Dag continued. "I am your chaperone, yah? Here to be ensuring safety and happiness for all childrens?" Once she'd volleyed that lie, she launched into an address that was intended to cow me with its volume and intensity. Respect for wildlife, check. Stupid blathering about curses, check. Reminders that she was the authority here and I was a mere child, check. General snottiness designed to make me feel like a dung ball a scarab might roll, check, check, check all the way to the bottom of the page. By the speech's end my head was reeling. It was also starting to feel a little baked as the Egyptian sun inched its way over the top of the mess tent.

"Got it," I said when she took an opportunity to breathe. "You betcha, coach."

Oops. Wrong word. I could tell as soon as it left my mouth. Her left eyebrow flew up as if it were counter-weighted to a heavy pulley. "Chaperone," she said in a tone chipped out of dry ice. "Now is time to be dressing. We have full day ahead. You, new young boy, I show you to your tent," she added. The new kid stood behind her, shifting his weight under his heavy backpack. An iPod was strapped to his waist, but its small earphones had been tucked into a pants pocket. The boy had been staring at me all through Dag's speech, but it was only at that moment that I once more noticed him.

When our eyes met, I stood still, stunned. My flesh had turned to stone.

"Well, I think it's terrible that Rona McDonald's always on your case," said Sunita, watching the chaperone stir up clouds of dust on her march back to camp. "And that Kathy Klemper is a snitch. You know how she got here? Her father's one of those University of Seattle professors, that's why."

"So's mine," I told her, barely able to work out the words. I couldn't tear my gaze from the boy's brown eyes. Curly brown hair spilled from under his backward-facing baseball cap onto the nape of his neck. "Oh, my God," I whispered. It was Connor Marsh. Connor Marsh was here in Luxor? And there I was, looking like . . . oh, man. Probably awful, in my sloppy sweats and my short black hair hanging every which way.

Deidre Pierce stepped in front of me, her thick dark eyebrows scrunched together in the middle, momentarily obscuring my view. "I wish I were like you," she admitted to me, hugging herself tight. "I just get *scared* of stuff like that. Why don't you ever get *scared?*"

Her words stabbed right to my gut. I couldn't let it show, though. "Aw, heck, it's nothing, really."

Bo Mereness clapped me on the back so hard that I nearly followed the scorpion over the cliff. He always talked to me like I was some kind of local hero. "Clo-meister! That was even better than when you were, like, the only one who crossed that humongous burial shaft when we went on that tour the first night. Remember? You're amazing!"

Remember? How could I forget? I could have been living a life of luxury down at the old monastery with the kids on the conservation team if I hadn't been the only Dig Egypt! kid to sprint across a two-by-four laid across the dark shaft on our first night. It was only when I looked back and saw none of the other kids following me that I realized I'd done something unusual. "She's supposed to be with conservation? No way—she's definitely one of ours," archaeologist Eddie Loret had said to Anca Battista, despite the fact that I wanted to scream at the thought of being on the excavation team for the rest of my stay.

The twins were sons of the project's rarely seen director, Dr. Tousson. They helped out the conservation team. I had twin brothers at home who were an awful lot alike, but these guys were uncannily similar—twin hunks who'd both gotten more than their share of the hottie gene. Mmmm, had they ever! I think I was catching on to the trick of telling them apart, though. Cyrus was the dark-skinned eighteen-year-old sex bomb with the thick eyebrows and long hair and the buffed-out chest and white, white teeth and sexy smile whom all the adults adored; he was supposed to be a genius of some kind. Seth was the dark-skinned eighteen-year-old sex bomb with the thick eyebrows and long hair and the buffed-out chest and white, white teeth and sexy smile who was supposed to be the bad boy of the two. Apart from each other, they were impossible to distinguish. "You are not like most American girls," said He-Who-I-Thought-Might-Be-Cyrus. I hoped it was a compliment. I wanted to melt at his smile, at his long braid, and at his beautiful, beautiful brown eyes. "You are . . . extraordinary."

Even the way he said *extraordinary* sounded extraordinary. "Oh, it's nothing," I said, bluffing it off and hoping he didn't notice my blush. Having Cyrus so much as notice me was making my insides squirmy. I mean, it even hurt to look at the guy, he was so hottilicious. Why hadn't I stopped to put on some lip gloss before I left the tent? Stupid, stupid Chloe!

He bowed his head at me and walked away. " 'Bye . . . Cy," I said, not saying the name very loudly. Had that been Cyrus? Or Seth? While I watched him go, I craned my neck to catch sight of Connor again. I could see only the back of his T-shirt, though, splashed with a big number 2, as he followed Dagmar and Kathy Klemper.

"Nothing!" said Bo. "You lie! That was ab-so-frickin'-lutely ab-so-mazing!"

"That twin is so seriously gorgeous," Deidre whispered. "I would have *fainted* if he talked to me."

She wasn't kidding. She really would have fainted. "Which one was he?" I asked her.

"Ohmigod, who cares?" Sue whispered to me. "He *talked* to you!" To Mallorie she explained, "*Le bel homme a parlé à mon mate du* tent!" Mallorie looked as dubious as ever.

The five of us started shuffling our way back to camp. The sounds of people rousing themselves and getting ready for a day's work were louder now. The rusty water tank was creaking ominously, the way it did when its water supply got low—which was always. And over it all I could smell sausages for breakfast.

I wasn't hungry at all, though. I couldn't even stomach the thought of food, or of washing the grit from my face with the half cup of water I'd be allotted for the day. All I could think about was Connor—a boy I already knew. Who was from my school. Who was only a grade ahead of me.

And who was going to bring everything I'd hoped to change about myself crashing down around me? Connor Marsh. Because the voice in my dream had been dead right. I was a total and utter fake, and he was the one person who would know it.

Two

I was no hero. No way, no how. I was the biggest coward alive, only bluffing my way through this miserable experience minute by minute, expecting anytime now to be caught. I was such a chicken liver, avoiding any strange experience, that my family had a nickname for me: Chloe, Queen of Denial.

It's true. I said no to everything. It didn't help my brothers were afraid of nothing. Next to them I was serious wimp material. If my family visited an amusement park, I would be the one miserably sitting on the benches all afternoon while Walter, Jesse, Ryan and the parents rode on the scary rides. The carousel I could handle. Roller coasters, twisty rides, and fast things—no. Conversations with strangers—no. Getting into trouble with the teachers—no way! Airplanes—no. Spiders, water slides, and giving talks in front of my class—no, no, and definitely not. I was miserable at scary movies. I couldn't even watch *The Wizard of Oz* all the way through until I was twelve, thanks to the green-faced witch. I still had to close my eyes and hunker down in the backseat of the family car whenever we drove over a bridge.

It was while I was in Tekhen and Tekhnet's tomb the afternoon of my scorpion incident that I realized I could blame this whole mess—scorpions, Egypt, dirty hair, filthy skin, every nasty thing that had happened to me in the last week—on Rose Kingsberry. It sounds silly to blame everything wrong in my life on a little fourth grader. It's even true that before she got me into this mess, I kind of liked the kid. Rose was one of the children in the after-school enrichment center where I spent two afternoons a week. You know, a rec room in the community center where a few girls and guys my age volunteered to lead latchkey kids in learning activities so they wouldn't have to go home and sit in an empty house all by themselves. It was one of the things my dad made me do because it would "look good on my college résumé," whatever that meant.

I'd been working on my college résumé since birth. I took Latin, I played Satan's sport for girls (a.k.a. lacrosse), I spent an hour every Sunday afternoon pounding out hymns on the piano at the Brook Haven Home for old folks. Even though I thought it sounded like a dying sheep, I played oboe in the school and in the citywide youth orchestras. During the summers, instead of kicking back at the community center pool with the rest of my friends, I spent three months in various programs at my dad's university, learning beginning Russian and getting instruction on elementary videotape technique or taking acting lessons and, of course, volunteering in the after-school enrichment center. Yeah, yeah, I know it was broadening. Yeah, I know it was good for me and someday waaaaaaay in the future I'd be happy to know how to say the Russian alphabet. Like, when I was a contestant on *Jeopardy!*, maybe.

All I wanted to do, though, was just relax once in a while. The enrichment center thing wasn't bad, though. I loved the kids. And Rose Kingsberry was cute as a button, with her velvety brown skin and bright eyes. If only I'd known what I was getting into when she came to me one Thursday afternoon and asked, "I have to write a report on pyramids. What's a pyramid?"

Well, I knew what a pyramid was. I'd been fascinated with ancient Egypt since I was a kid. I watched all the shows on the Discovery Channel about it. I'd read books. Okay, to be perfectly honest, I'd opened books and skipped over the words so I could look at all the pictures of gold treasures and ruined artifacts and of all the statues with the crazy dog heads.

For two weeks I showed Rose all kinds of pictures of pyramids and how they'd been made. Then one day she pointed to the hieroglyphics in one of the books. "What do these do?" she wanted to know. I told her that was how the ancient Egyptians wrote. "That's not *real* writing." You've never heard a fourth grader so scornful.

"Sure it is," I said. "Let me show you how it works."

And that's the moment my trouble began.

Working with people younger than me wasn't scary at all. Mrs. Pillsby, who ran the enrichment center, basically let me take over the place while I taught the kids about hieroglyphics. Sure, it's a kind of picture writing, but each one of those pictures stands for a *sound,* I told them. For two days I helped them make their own hieroglyphics to represent their name. "Think about your name," I told Rose. "What picture can represent the sounds of it?"

"Picture?" she asked. Suddenly she got a big goofy grin on her face and used a Crayola to draw a flower with thorns sticking out of its stem. "Cool," I told her. "Now your last name?" After a long period of thought, she decided on a royal circlet with pointy spikes and then three round fruits with joined stems that looked like they should have been on a slot machine. Okay, so anyone might have thought her name was Thorny Crowncherry, but when she was done, she totally got it.

So did all the other kids. Mrs. Pillsby and I went around the little tables one by one, though, and helped them dream up pictures to represent the sounds in their names. Then we'd write them in a vertical column and surround them with an oval to make cartouches, just like the Egyptians used to represent an important name. Some of them were harder than others, mind you. I can't even tell you the gymnastics I went through to help kids like Alanna Chlebnik. Rose helped too. She seemed pleased as punch to be one of the teachers in the exercise, and that made *me* feel like I'd actually accomplished something.

Then she went and told her dad on me.

It was one of those normal dinners at home, mid-July. Mom and I were talking about who'd been kicked off a reality TV show the night before. I could tell something was up, though, when my dad answered the phone and spent over fifteen minutes talking, one hand over his ear so he could hear better. His eyes never left me except to give my mom significant looks. "Mmmm-hmmm," he would say. "Mmmm-hmmm." He stayed on the line until we'd cleared our plates and I'd curled up on the sofa with a book, and then he and Mom went into the bedroom together and had a long, long talk.

It was two days later that they sat down opposite me in the living room. "Do you know Rose Kingsberry?" my dad asked.

"Sure, from enrichment," I said, not realizing I was sealing my fate.

"Her dad, Wilbur, teaches at the university. Anthropology. Different department from me, but he knew my name and called to tell me you held quite the little teaching session at the center last week. Care to tell me about it?"

Was I in trouble? Was Dr. Kingsberry upset that people thought his daughter was named Crowncherry? I stammered out an account of what I'd done. Dad gave Mom one of those parental looks. I wish someone would make a Parent/Normal Person–Normal Person/Parent translation dictionary.

Then I heard Dad proclaim my doom. "Well, this is the thing, honey," he said. "This autumn, the University of Seattle is the academic sponsor for a really special nationwide opportunity for kids your age. It's called Dig Egypt! You'd get to spend a whole month at an excavation site in the Valley of the Servitors, working on either the excavation or conservation of the . . ." He consulted the brochure. "The tomb of Tekhen and Tekhnet."

"In Egypt," my mom echoed, trying to be helpful and excited. I just gaped at her. Oh, believe me, I knew where the Valley of the Servitors was.

"And because of your hieroglyphics class, he's nominated you to go," my dad explained. I could tell he was trying to be as gentle as possible.

"It's really an honor," said my mother. Then they sat back and waited for my reaction.

What was my reaction? Horror. Absolute, chill-in-my-heart horror. "No," I croaked.

"Sweetie—" said Mom.

"Your mother and I agree it would look good on your college résumé," Dad said.

I shook my head. Go to Egypt? All the way across the world? *Go to Egypt?* "No!"

I should have known what my dad was going to say

then. "Well, here she comes. Right on schedule! Our own little Queen of Denial." That was how everyone knew me. Chloe the scaredy-cat. Chloe, Queen of Denial. Chloe the spoilsport. His words stung, but I couldn't contradict them. There was too much past evidence against me.

"I can't do anything like that," I told him. My intestines felt like someone had loaned them to a Boy Scout troop for knot-tying practice. I wanted to gnaw at my fingernails, but I knew my mother would just grab my hand from my mouth. "I just can't. Please don't ask me. I can't."

Against my dad and his dreams of my college résumé, I didn't stand a chance. Because you know, colleges were going to think it was oh-so-glamorous that for a solid month I squatted down in the vestibule of an Egyptian tomb in a pile of rubble with a sieve, looking for little shards of pottery.

I liked the vestibule. It was just off the main entrance room, close enough to the entrance that when I felt like the walls were closing in on me, I could step outside for some fresh, nostril-burning air. From time to time, some of the Egyptian workers would pass through on their way from the tomb's far end, hauling rubber baskets of sifted rubble to deposit outdoors.

"Yo, Clo." One of the Tousson twins stuck his head out of the narrow passageway that led to the antechamber. "Come look at this. I think you'll get a kick out of it."

I would have taken any excuse to get out of my own personal gravel pit at that point. Squatting made my legs cramp. Plus there was the fact that I was seeing imaginary scorpions everywhere I looked, now. Besides, was I going to give up a chance to get a little flirty with one of the two guys we girls had elected hottest hotties of the camp? Nuh-uh. Scaredy-cat I might be, but I wasn't stupid. "What's happening?" I asked.

Although outside, beyond the squat entrance of the tomb, the sun was shining in a way that made me want to fall down to my knees and beg for mercy not much of it illuminated past the tall and narrow vestibule. Every few feet a couple of electric utility lamps cast their glare up onto the stone, connected by thick bundles of electrical cord that snaked their way through the entrance to the gas-powered generator that chugged away outdoors. I squeezed through the narrow passageway to the dark vestibule, where the twin was straddling his ladder with one leg on either side. Which one was he? It had to be Cyrus. This guy was definitely the same one who talked to me that morning, of that much I was certain. Cy was wearing a tight muscle tee that showed off his biceps. And triceps. And pectorals. And deltoids. Suddenly I wondered if I needed a drool bucket. "Come look," he told me as he climbed his ladder. "It's awesome."

His hand cast a long, strange shadow on the wall when he reached down to help me up. One of the things I most hated about my situation was that I had to *think* all the time about how brave people reacted to things, and then do what they'd do. Instinct normally made me shy away from ladders, and dark places, and narrow hallways, and cramped quarters. Grim determination was the only thing that made me put my foot onto the first rung and accept his grasp. I was almost instantly grateful I did; my little fingers felt so huge in his big paw that it felt like holding hands with a hunky Goliath.

Once I managed to get three-quarters of the way up the ladder, I was surprised how close I stood to him. Instinct made me want to climb back down again, and in a hurry. Determination—and the squiggly feeling inside my tummy—made me stay. I tried to act cool, though. I tried to ignore the way he stared at me and squeezed my hand. I kept my mouth from saying the word *no.* "So what did you want to show me?" I heard myself saying. To my horror, I sounded almost flirtatious. Me? Flirtatious? With an older guy? No way! That had to be someone else speaking!

"Hmmm!" Cy smirked at me, like he thought I was being flirty as well . . . and liked it. The sound was like a cattle prod to my skin. I wanted to yank my hand back and run. But I let him hold it. "Look at these," he said.

Cy had been cleaning four thousand years' worth of grime from a portion of the antechamber wall. A big step up from my dirt-sifting on the excavation team, but then again, that's the kind of easy work the conservation team got to do all day. Yes, I was the only sixteen-year-old in existence with an ulcerated stomach from flying halfway across the world so she could be chambermaid to the ancients. When I let go of Cy's hand, his long fingers moved to a section of the smooth, plastered wall that wasn't black with centuries of soot and grime and dust. With a gentle tapping motion, he cleared away a last smudgy bit using his crumbly sponge, and I saw what he'd brought me over for.

"Oh, my gosh," I whispered. I stepped up another rung on the ladder to take a closer look. Monkeys! The paint was as vibrant and colorful as the day it had been painted. Cy had been cleaning a section of white plaster painted with . . . well, I guess it was a dinner scene. There was a table, certainly, and at either end of it sat two stern-looking Egyptian gals with the same hair and the same reddish-brown skin and profile. Tekhen and Tekhnet, presumably. They looked like sisters having a conversation over the dinner table. Their long necks inclined toward each other and their bracelet-decorated wrists stuck out in weird Walk-like-an-Egyptian angles. The real action, however, was happening on the side, where little ancient monkeys were totally stealing the scene. Two of them were eating loaves of bread. Two more sat underneath the table, tickling each other, it looked like. Others had been painted off to the sides, watching. Surrounding the scene were scads of hieroglyphics.

I couldn't help but laugh. The entire scene was like nothing I'd ever seen before. "You conservation team guys have all the fun," I told him. "Nice quarters, more water, no scorpions. Very cool. You should show one of the archaeologists." I took a step down.

"Wait," Cy told me, grabbing my hand once more. "Is there a rush?"

The way he stared made me pause. "There doesn't have to be." Again, my voice came out differently than I thought it would. Mischievous. Teasing, even.

He looked embarrassed. Maybe I'd overdone it. I was about to run away in shame when he said, face glum, "I was thinking that perhaps you might give me a kiss before you head down again."

Yikes! I started to get all trembly again, and prayed that my suddenly sweaty palms wouldn't give me away. "How about I not?" I said, grinning at him. For a moment I thought I smelled the incense of millennia gone by, until I realized the perfume came from Cy's skin. It was funny how all of a sudden, over the dusty smells of the tomb, I noticed how Cy had a scent of his own. It was slightly musty and damp, like my brothers' laundry in the dirty clothes hamper, but there was mostly sharp sweetness, like aftershave, and a hint of leather.

Cy leaned closer and parted his lips. My own instinctively

moved closer. "Tell me," he murmured. "Do I look gay to you?"

"What? No!" My lips retreated again. What the heck?

"*Ja*—well, someone said she thought I was gay."

I narrowed my eyes a little. Was that what this was all about? "You want me to kiss you because someone said you looked gay?"

Cy seemed genuinely confused. "She called me a *dawg* too, I believe." The word sounded strange coming from his lips. "And a player. What does it mean to be a player?"

"Whoever she is," I said, wholeheartedly condemning the fool, "she's crazy."

"I thought so too. Wait," he said when I started to climb down. "How about the kiss?"

"Hey, what part of ankh-next-to-vulture-over-squiggly-line don't you understand?" I joked as he moved even closer. Inside my head, though, I was running over what might happen if I were to say yes. I don't know what frightened me more, the actual prospect of kissing someone as beautiful as Cy . . . or never getting another chance.

That thought decided me. I closed my eyes and took a deep breath, and didn't protest when he finally raised my chin up to his own, tilted it slightly, and pressed his lips against mine. I couldn't believe how gentle his lips were, or how soft they felt as they pressed against my own.

"Wow," I said when the kiss was over. His technique had been a perfect ten. But . . . I don't know. It had felt more like a science lab experiment than real making out. It just didn't have spark.

The electric light flooding up from below seemed to make his eyes sparkle. "Yeah. Wow."

"Yeah, wow, you guys." The voice came from below, and

I almost fell off the ladder in surprise. I had been so over-whelmed by the kiss that I had completely failed to notice an archaeologist and a few other kids from the project now standing beneath us. Eddie Loret, second-in-command of the excavation team, had his arms crossed and his teeth bared in what wasn't exactly a grimace, but wasn't exactly a smile of joy, either.

"The heck!" I exclaimed, backing down the ladder with a speed that I didn't have to fake.

"Oh, no, don't let me interrupt you two," said Eddie in a cheerful manner. He uncrossed his arms and rubbed the palms of his hands together. "I know that in the dark an-techamber of a necropolis, out of the rays of the hot sun, it can get a touch chilly. Chilly enough to send a girl into the arms of a warm boy. After all, it must be a nippy eighty-five degrees in here, huh?"

Eddie was basically a good sort, for an old guy in his thir-ties. His joke eased my embarrassment a little bit, but not by much, especially when I saw that crushed in the narrow room stood the following people:

1) Dr. Jumoke, one of the Egyptian representatives from the Supreme Council of Antiquities who were always there to make sure that no one dam-aged anything valuable
2) Connor Marsh, his hands in his pockets, staring at the floor and back at the entrance and at the ceil-ing and at Eddie. Anywhere, in other words, but in my direction
3) Kathy Klemper, who looked as if she'd sat on a pharaoh's scepter and forgotten to pull it out of her butt, and

25

4) Cyrus's twin, Seth, grinning his head off. You know, boys really just don't know the meaning of the word *discreet*.

Wait a minute. Wait one diddly-darn minute. The twin on the floor wasn't Seth at all. It wasn't until I saw the two of them in the room that I realized Cyrus, everyone's favorite archaeological genius, the one wearing khakis like Eddie, was the twin who'd just entered the room.

That meant the twin in the muscle tee was . . . I looked back up the ladder at the guy I'd just kissed. "Wait. You're Seth?" I asked him.

A flash of annoyance crossed his face when he realized I'd mistaken him for his brother. "Didn't you even know who I was?" he complained.

"Duh! Sure I did!" It was a big fat lie.

"It's just disgusting," Kathy commented to Connor, "how *some* people on their Dig Egypt! excursion are over-looking a magnificent educational opportunity in favor of promiscuous teenage sex."

I hadn't even known whom I was kissing! How embarrassing was that? Humiliated as I felt, I didn't plan to let it show. That's not the kind of person I was, out here in the desert. "How many candles should I put on your next birthday cake?" I blurted out to Kathy. "Sixty? Who *talks* like that?"

"Now, now," said Eddie Loret. I liked Eddie. Whenever he talked to the teens working on Dig Egypt!, it was easy to forget that he was second-in-command to Anca Battista. She was all business; he was friendly and approachable. I couldn't imagine Dr. Battista making a joke, ever; Eddie always had one at the ready. Anca Battista was like the Great and Powerful Oz right before he made the Cowardly Lion hightail it out of the Emerald City palace; Eddie was like one of my big brothers dressed up in Indiana Jones gear. "No duking it out, you two. At least . . . not until the rest of the camp is here! Hey everyone, *girl fight!*" he yelled down the antechamber corridor at the top of his voice, his hands cupped together around his mouth.

"Hah," I told him, putting my hands on my hips. "Not funny." It was bad enough I was still mortified about having my kiss witnessed. I didn't need joking on top of it.

"That's not funny at all," Kathy Klemper snarled at the same time. We stared at each other. I think she was just as astonished we'd actually agreed about something.

"Eddie, I think you'll appreciate what's up here," said Seth from the top of the ladder. I had to give him credit: He didn't seem at all embarrassed about being found in a lip-lock with me. It's different for boys, though—I think they'd even do the bedroom stuff in public if some other guy was around to high-five them afterward.

Eddie lurched forward like he was going to sprint right up the ladder, then jerked to a halt. "No can do, Seth, man," he said. "I've got to take a few documents down to the boss lady before showing our new guy around the site some more, and I'm already on a tight schedule here." He seemed genuinely regretful. I knew from my own dad's yearlong experience as department chair of the classics department that once you move up in the administration, it's all running around and paperwork and none of the fun stuff anymore.

"Hey," I said, struck by a thought. "Why don't I run the stuff down to Dr. Battista? You can check out the paintings up there and everyone's happy." Everyone would be happy except me, that is. The minuses of this trip all centered around the terrifying trip down to the burial chamber. Tight spaces. Darkness. And hello! Mummies! There was a single plus, though. Running the errand would help me get away from Kathy, get away from Connor, and flee the scene of my shame.

Eddie actually beamed at me. "Grand idea!" From over his shoulder he unlooped a document tube and handed it to me. I could hear the papers shifting inside. "Marsh . . . follow our intrepid young Ms. Bryce, would you? She's one of our natural-born leaders." He clapped Connor on the shoulder as he spoke. I wanted to shriek. No! I was supposed to be *fleeing* Connor. Not giving him a guided tour!

"I'll go with them." Kathy spoke the same way that a preschool teacher might if two of her three-year-olds had suggested they could cross a crowded street all by themselves. I half expected her to add, *Crazy children!*

"Well, all right then," said Eddie, finally climbing the ladder. Noooooooo! I wanted to be miserable on my own! "But you two stay up on this level. Chloe knows her way around a ladder. Right?" The wink he gave me, followed by Kathy's expression of squashed triumph, was more than ample reward for having to chauffeur through the tomb the two people in camp I least wanted to spend time with.

"I like the monkeys tickling each other the best," I called up to Eddie as he started to inspect the wall.

"It's really unique," I heard Seth ask him. "Isn't it?"

"Not so very," said Cy in a tone of authority. "Monkeys were found in the funerary inscriptions of the tomb of the seventeenth-dynasty governor Sobeknakht of Upper Egypt."

"Hey, Chloe?" Eddie called from the top of the ladder, making a funny noise. It kind of sounded like he was trying not to laugh. "You know those tickling monkeys of yours? Well, they're kinda . . . sorta . . . mating."

28

I heard Seth snort. "Come on," I told the terrible two-some, trying to sound carefree. I hustled out of the antechamber before I could find out anything more about the monkeys' monkey business.

It's hard to describe what I have to do to keep the Queen of Denial squashed. You see, when I realized I had no choice and that I had to come out to Egypt because if I didn't, my father would skin me alive, shoot me full of elephant tranquilizers, and then nail me in a big crate and ship me to spend October in the desert just for one more bullet point on my college résumé, I knew I had to give my attitude a makeover.

So I decided to become someone else. Someone braver than me. Someone *better* than me. She might have shared my name and clothes, but she wasn't a chicken liver. The better me spoke up when she didn't want to. She went first. She didn't think about ladders or snakes or about all the things that made her insides hurt and her head ache and her shoulders hunch over in fear. She just *did* stuff. On the plane she sat quietly and read a book and slept and didn't twitch and annoy the flight attendants by howling every time the landing gear made noises. On the trip from Cairo to Luxor, she didn't scream every time the van lurched into a bottomless pothole and broke her tailbone. And at camp, when she looked around and saw a bunch of tired, miserable kids, some of whom were more frightened than she was, she gritted her teeth, clamped down on her squirming stomach, and hid the Queen of Denial deep inside, in an airtight little box where no one would ever know she existed.

While I led them out of the antechamber and into the vestibule, Kathy kept up a preachy monologue swiped straight from Rona McDonald's canned list of lectures.

"What we have learned so far about this tomb is that it was built during the—"

"Yeah, the eighteenth dynasty," I heard Connor say.

"That's right. The Valley of the Servitors' cliff tombs are unusual, since most honored servants were interred in mastabas. A mastaba is a flat-roofed burial chapel built by the ancient Egyptians for—"

"I know what a mastaba is, thanks." Well! Connor sounded a mite impatient, there! Maybe he disliked a showoff, too.

You could always tell the excavation team members from the conservation team. We were filthy. They were clean. Some of the conservationists we passed wore miner's helmets with lights in them, so that they could lay sheets of thick transparent plastic over the hieroglyphics on the walls and then trace the symbols one by one. Every time one of the adults called my name with a friendly shout or a smile, it surprised me. I wasn't used to being liked, or admired, or even noticed. Invisible—now, that I was used to. Invisible I could do with my eyes closed.

I nearly jumped out of my skin when I felt a hand on my shoulder. "Hey." It was Connor, catching up with me. "I know you, right? I think I do."

The scaredy-cat in me scratched and roared to get out. "Yeah." I wrenched my shoulder from his grasp. Was that abrupt enough? "Hey, January," I called out to a girl with curly red hair standing at the foot of a ladder. Jan James was one of the two Dig Egypt! kids lucky enough to be on the conservation team. She and Izumi were chattering while Izumi used little dry-clean sponges to remove grit and grime from the walls, just as Seth had been doing. "Hi, Izumi."

"Hey, um, you!" Jan smiled back.

Jan was quasi-friendly, but I realized she didn't remember my name. A safe distance away, I pushed my finger against the tip of my nose to raise it up. "Preservation is *so* full of snobs," I murmured to Connor. We started to descend the rough-hewn stone staircase down. I still felt a little guilty about how gruff I'd been with him, so I added, "We're both at North Seattle High, right?"

"You two *know* each other?" Kathy asked. She didn't sound at all happy, but even the frightened kid in me didn't give a flying flip.

"Oh, yeah," I heard Connor behind me. "That's where I remember you from!" I dreaded the rest. *You're the one who couldn't dive in gym because the board was too high. You're the one who doesn't go to dances because you're scared people will talk about you. You're the one everybody's laughing at behind your back because you're too frightened to do anything!* Instead he said only, "You hang out with . . . Baz Wilder. Right?"

Me? Hang out with the most popular eleventh grader ever invented? Baz's little clique was crazy. They partied until all hours of the night, cut class, and had connections with all the cool seniors. Baz and his friends were the chosen disciples, the ones who'd inherit the school once the twelfth graders hit the road, diplomas in hand. And I'd be one of the kids they'd wipe their boots on when it happened. Hang out with Baz Wilder? Not likely!

I was about to say no when something occurred to me. Connor thought I was part of the popular set? Really? Me? How weird. But why?

Because I wasn't acting like a cringing little mouse with a KICK ME! sign attached to her back, I realized. Because I was acting like a winner and not a loser.

What did I even know about Connor Marsh? Not much.

I'd heard he lived in Australia for a year. I knew he'd transferred into North Seattle High last January, and that he had been one of the state science fair winners in the spring. I didn't think he was part of any particular set of kids.

Here I'd assumed from the moment Connor showed up, he'd spill the beans about how I really was. It never had occurred to me he simply didn't have beans to spill. "You know," I told him, my confidence rebounding, "I don't really hang out with anybody. People hang out with *me.*" The three of us stepped into the dark and undecorated room where the shaft to the burial chamber lay. "Play your cards right, and I'll let you be one of them." Did that sound cocky? Did I care?

He seemed surprised at my words, but the moment he nodded, I knew I had him hooked. Score one for new, confident Chloe!

"Play cards with *her* and you'll get a scorching case of scabby lips," Kathy murmured.

I pretended not to hear. "The floorplan of this place isn't too difficult, but if you get turned around, find the electrical cords," I told him, pointing to the bundle that snaked along the floor and then disappeared into the depths below. "You can follow them back to the entrance."

The burial shaft room was one of the darkest in the entire tomb. The shaft itself was a gaping hole in the hallway's center, barely visible in the shadows. Spikes supporting a rope ladder had been hammered into the rock floor. It was a huge contrast to the hole I'd crossed on a two-by-four our first night here. That tomb's shaft had crumbled and disintegrated through the centuries until it was more like a gaping mouth to hell; this was more a friendly little shaft that I was going to scoot down, I told the Queen of Denial. A cozy little hole. Not a constrictive, claustrophobic chamber of death where suddenly the sands above me could shift and collapse and I could find myself choking to death, gasping for air, praying for one more second to my life as I plummeted thirty feet down to certain death. Yeah. Just a friendly, cozy little—

I gulped.

"What's the matter? Scared?" Kathy's voice was so shrill it could have curdled cow brains.

I turned around and made an elaborate show of rolling my eyes. "Gosh, Kathy, I'm just plain ol' terrified," I mocked, pretending to shiver and quake. I could have kicked her right then for nailing what made me pause. "Maybe I should be like you and get Dag to hold my hand."

Connor turned his baseball cap around and snorted at my comment; I almost wanted to hug him for that. He cleared his throat. "I thought we weren't supposed to go down there. That's what Ms. Sorensson . . . Dag . . . said."

"Yeah, well, if we did everything that Swedish meatball said, we wouldn't have any fun around here." I enjoyed the look on Kathy's face at that remark.

"You'll be okay?" he asked.

"Please. Of course," I said, hauling the document tube's strap over my shoulder and sitting down on the edge of the oblong shaft. *"No problemo."* While Kathy stood back against the wall with her arms and eyes crossed—okay, the last was just wishful thinking on my part—Connor leaned over and held my hand while I hooked my feet onto the rope ladder and twisted around. "Thanks," I told him, grateful he'd been there. Somehow he'd made it all easier.

"No problemo," he repeated, and let go of my hand.

I took a step down the ladder, the plastic cylinder banging against the stone behind me. *He's only being nice because he thinks you're popular,* a nasty voice said in the back of my head. I thought about that for a second, and decided I could live with it. Out here, I *was* popular.

Here's how the Queen of Denial coped with scary things in Luxor: She pretended they weren't happening. When I began the climb down that dusty, cramped hole, it felt as if my lungs were barely able to suck in half the oxygen they needed. Although the temperature dropped with every foot of my descent, the air seemed clammy and close instead of cool. The ladder rattled and swung loosely as if it could collapse at any moment . . . but I pretended to ignore all these things. Some moments in my life I simply needed to endure. I could endure anything, right? When you're a coward at heart, life hands you so many moments that are just sheer misery. You block them out. You grit your teeth and pretend they're not happening—because everything's temporary, after all.

The bottom of the ladder dangled down into the rock chamber and scraped against the bedrock floor of the chamber below. When I stepped off, it wasn't with a sense of relief. I had only given up one claustrophobic enclosure for another. I'd never been down in the burial chamber before; I'm not sure what I was expecting, but it wasn't a low-ceilinged, stuffy cavern in which I could barely stand upright, piled with debris that came up to my shoulders. This wasn't a fabulous *Raiders of the Lost Ark* set. Someone had plunked me in the Ashtray of the Egyptian Damned.

Over on the far side of the room, Dr. Battista stood hunched over a sarcophagus. There was so very little light that it was nearly impossible to see my way across the rubble on the floor. Two archaeologists from the excavation team crowded in on either side; one held the only lantern over the dark basalt tomb. The light streamed upward, past their faces, illuminating them like mad scientists hovering over a reanimated monster on the slab. Their long shadows streamed over the wall beyond, where an engraving of the god Anubis towered. Its jackal head was sinister and forbidding. The sight made me stumble over a gravel patch, fall to my butt, and slam the plastic tube against my head with a hollow bonk. Dr. Battista's head jerked up. "Who's there?" barked one of her assistants.

Well, sheesh. You would've thought I was a CGI effect straight out of Industrial Light and Magic, a mummy with blazing eyes and a jaw hanging by a thin thread of desiccated flesh, the way they reacted. I picked some gravel out of my rear and scooped myself back to my feet, comforting myself with the realization that they had been as frightened of me as I had been of them. "Just me," I said.

I realized how stupid that was the moment the words left my mouth. One of the junior archaeologists looked grumpy at having the moment interrupted. "Students are not allowed—"

"Wait." Dr. Battista peered through the darkness, trying to adjust her narrow, tiny eyes. Rumor around the camp was that her grandmother had been a gypsy. In the shadows, with her long, curly hair tied back, she looked more like a witch than a scientist. "Chloe Bryce, isn't it?"

A little shock thrilled me when I realized that Anca Battista actually remembered my name. I cleared my throat and held out the tube. "Eddie sent me down with . . ."

I meant to finish the sentence, but that's when I saw the dead lady. A mummified corpse of a woman lay inside the sarcophagus, exposed after thousands of years. Her eyes were thin, leathery slits. Her mouth was slightly agape, as if she were only sleeping. Little tufts of hair stuck out over her ears. She looked like my mom's boss, Mrs. Murphy, after a long, long bask in the Arizona desert sun. Say, a two-thousand-year bask, without moisturizer or SPF of any kind. The mummy's skin was leathery and dry, and her bones were thin and fragile, as if a single touch could reduce them to dust.

On the creepiness scale this was past Vincent Price in *House of Wax,* past *Nightmare on Elm Street,* even way, way past being taken to a Peter, Paul, and Mary concert by your parents and being coerced into clapping along with "Puff the Magic Dragon." Yes, I've been there. Shudder. Good-bye, hot Teflon pan! Hello, charbroiling flames! I flinched as my stomach started to clench.

"It's fine," said Dr. Battista. When she straightened up, she shook her long ponytail free of her neck. "Chloe's one of Dig Egypt!'s best and bravest." I tucked away the compliment to hug to myself later on. Now, though, I could only think about the mummy. My brain knew that the woman had been dead for thousands of years and that she was not, could not, was *not* suddenly going to lurch from the sarcophagus and uncross her arms and make banshee noises as she went for my neck.

At the same time, she was a dead person. A very ancient dead person. And Chloe the Frightened didn't like very ancient leathery dead people any more than she liked fresh and juicy dead people. Nuh-uh. No way.

Chloe the Frightened wasn't in control now, though. I stepped forward and looked over the edge of the sarcophagus, gulping down my fear and pretending to be interested. *You can endure anything,* I told myself. *This is only temporary.* "You are looking upon the mummy of Tekhen, Queen Nefertari's most honored servant. Amazing, isn't it?" Dr. Battista's voice echoed dully from the rock ceiling. "We are the first to look upon these women in four thousand years. Observe how the wrappings have been removed at some time in the past, probably by grave robbers looking for funerary gold." She continued pointing out the mummy's features to us, but somehow I thought she was talking directly to me.

Something about the tone of her voice suddenly made me take in the awe of the scene. Just a minute before I'd stood in a dusty, rocky pit, looking at a particularly creepy prop from a bad horror movie. When Dr. Battista spoke, I felt like I was in a museum—no, better than that. For the first time since I'd arrived in Egypt, I felt as if I were standing in the middle of history. In my imagination I could see the walls here as they once might have been, smooth and brightly painted and carved with hieroglyphics. I could almost smell the braziers of incense, hear the cries of the mourners as they processed through the meandering tomb bearing the sarcophagi.

"Wait a minute. What do you mean, 'these women'? This isn't a tomb built for two, is it?" I stepped back and casually leaned against a stone wall to put a little distance between myself and the grand prize winner of the 2000 B.C. *Newlydead Game.*

Dr. Battista quirked an eyebrow at me, and extended a long finger in the direction over my shoulder. I turned to see what she was pointing at.

That was no wall I'd been leaning on. It was another stone sarcophagus, twin to the first. Through the gloom I could see another leathery, desiccated face only inches away from my own. I gulped. "Oh. Sure. And what did you say these girls were, again?" I choked out.

When Dr. Battista pronounced their titles, I still didn't believe her.

37

Three

"Tekhen and Tekhnet? Those chicks were manicurists to Nefertari? I still can't get over it. *Twin* manicurists to the queen? I just think it's kind of . . . you know," said Bo. It was several days after my encounter in the tomb. He lifted his leg from the ground and brushed sand from it unconsciously. We all were brushing sand and dirt from our skin as we talked there in my tent. I hadn't realized how much I'd taken cleanliness for granted until going without baths for the last nine days. "Kind of *gay,* that's all."

When my mom and dad were trying to talk me into this so-called adventure, they kept pointing out the "amenities" in the university's brochure. "Look," they'd told me. "The kids in Dig Egypt! enjoy the same amenities as the archaeologists. Private and comfortable double occupancy accommodations, three hot meals daily, recreational facilities. . . ."

Fancy words for tents so old that I think they originally belonged to Alexander the Great's army, food prepared from just-add-water evaporated packets, and a Ping-Pong table plunked down at the side of a research trailer. Ping-Pong, recreational? The heck!

Chloe, Queen of Denial

At least each and every private double-occupancy accommodation came with a genuine photon-producing glass-encased personal illumination device—or as it's sometimes called in real English, a kerosene lantern. Its glow helped brighten the little circle where Sue and Deidre and Bo and Mallorie and I huddled, eating cake. There had been a big camp celebration for Mrs. Tousson's birthday in the mess tent, but we'd only gone long enough to grab some snacks. "Let me get your club and loincloth, Mr. Neanderthal," I said. "Just because Tekhen and Tekhnet were manicurists and you're excavating their tomb doesn't make you gay."

Mallorie, as usual, looked totally lost.

"*Les* mummies *du*, um, Lee Press-On? *Ne c'est pas* Bo how you say *avec* George Michael?" Sue explained.

"Yeah, grow up!" Deidre snapped at Bo. "It was a royal title!"

"Seriously," Sue agreed. "What's so funny about manicurists, anyway? Every ruler needs her nails done. *Un roi* needs her nails *du doigts attendez-vous à la* Christian Dior," she added for Mallorie's benefit. "Oh, wait. *Ongles.* I think that's fingernails. *Ongles, ongles,*" she said, pretending to claw at Mallorie's face.

Sue's werewolf imitation made poor Mallorie widen her big eyes and cringe back. "I really don't think you're getting through to that poor girl," I told Sue. "Unless, of course, you're trying to make her think we're all *insane.*"

"Whatever. You do the translating, then!" Sue seemed put out by my remark.

"All I know is that I didn't spend two whole weeks working on my essay and take a whole month off from school my sophomore year to come here for makeover tips. If I get all *Queer Eye for the Mummy Guy,* it's going to be this place's fault." Bo complained. Deidre made a snerking sound at that remark, then covered her mouth with her hand and pretended to be yawning instead.

"You wrote an essay to get into Dig Egypt!?" I asked Bo. I'm not sure which caught my attention more—the fact he'd had to write something, or the notion that Bo might do anything that didn't involve a joystick and an Xbox.

"Uh, yeah!" It was the *duh!* tone of voice that caught my attention. "One thousand words on why you feel Dig Egypt! would be important to you and why you would be important to Dig Egypt!"

"Didn't you write one?" Sue asked me, toying with the end of her long, dark braid. "I sure did." In a louder voice, she added to Mallorie, "*L'*essay *du mille bornes.*"

"Yeah, sure thing." It was a bold-faced lie. I hadn't written a word. I'd only taught fake hieroglyphics to the daughter of a guy in the department sponsoring the project and boom! Here I was in Egypt. Stupid of me, I know. Knowing that I'd been bumped to the head of the line without deserving it made me feel even more miserable about being here than before. "It just took me *three* weeks, that's all. *Trois,*" I said to Mallorie. "*Trois.*"

"It is so freakin' hot," said Deidre, fanning herself. "I haven't showered since I got here."

"None of us have," I reminded her. "We're all messes."

"I bet Izumi and Jan aren't messes," Bo said. We'd all been thinking the same thing, I'm sure. "I bet they're both happy in their little off-site monastery."

"Clean, too," said Deidre with a sigh.

"The monastery has its own well," said Sue, adding, "*La compagnie de la* conservation has their own hole *de l'eau à la maison du* monks.*"

Our excavation camp had its water tank refilled twice

daily by a truck that traveled several miles from the monastery; the water had to be shared with site archaeologists, the kids on our team, the mess tent, and all the Egyptian workers camping at the site. "Yeah, they don't have all their water rations sucked up by Dag, either. I swear she and Kathy are taking baths and doing laundry just about every day," I told them. "Um, *lavage*," I explained to Mallorie, making a scrubbing motion with my hands.

"Can't we report her?" Deidre asked. "It was my turn to wash clothes this morning, but when I got to the tank it only dribbled at me."

"And *she* turned up looking all fresh and clean," Bo said. "I saw her. Clo, you've got to tell someone."

Why me? The downside of everyone thinking you're brave, I'd found out, was that everyone considers you a leader. Which is totally unfair, if you want one without the other. "I'll think about it." Outside the tent I could hear gravel crunching. I held up a finger. "Ssssh, it might be Kathy or Dag," I warned the others. Then, to change the topic, "You know the conservation kids look down on us."

"They call us grunts," Bo said. "I heard Jan say it, and I was like, 'Dude, even with that rack, you're not all that!'"

"Rack!" I protested. "Bo, that's awful. Never, ever, *ever* use that word!"

"Forget rack. Excuse me? *Grunts?* Just because our butts aren't pampered?" asked Sue.

I let her grapple with the challenge of translating that one. "I don't even think they've bothered learning our names." At most, Izumi and Jan had been icily polite. "Snobs."

"If it weren't for us, they wouldn't have anything to conserve," said Bo. "If I have to hear them talk about *their* fabulous treasures one more time . . ."

"Now, now," I interrupted, giving a good imitation of Dr. Battista's stern tones. "We archaeologists are not in the business for *treasure,* but for *information.* There is as much to be learned about a culture from their pottery shards as from their jewelry and riches."

"We're the ones who dig out those pottery shards."

"That's for sure," Sue said. Everyone nodded their heads. Mallorie joined in as well, just to be part of the crowd. I felt so sorry for her that I reconsidered eating the second slice of cake I'd brought back with me, and gave it to her instead. She beamed as I passed it over. "Besides, we're a *much* more interesting group. *Anyone* can be on the preservation team."

" 'Syeah," Sue agreed. "*La compagnie du* dig-dig *es muy interesante.*"

Bo looked pained. "Like, even I know some of that was Spanish."

"How do you like finally having a tentmate?" I asked him. "Is Connor cool?"

"Yeah, he's cool. Little bit geeky, but cool," Bo admitted. I was willing to bet his reluctance came from having to give up his solo tent for a late-arriving roommate. "He's always reading. I don't get why he came three days after us, though. I mean, that university gave him a scholarship. You think he'd have been out here the first day."

"Yeah, I don't know what's up with that," I admitted. "Where is he, anyway? I hope he's not hanging out with Kathy Klemper."

Even Mallorie shuddered at Kathy's name. I suppose some things transcend all languages. "Last time I saw the dude, he was hanging out on the plateau ledge. Reading, of course." Bo seemed a little scornful at that. "Okay, I brought the cards. Who's up for Hearts?"

"*Coeurs?*" Sue asked Mallorie, who nodded vigorously. At least card games didn't necessarily require her to speak our language.

"You guys play," I told them. "I'm going to take a walk."

Part of me felt gratified that they groaned over my decision to sit out. Popularity was something I just wasn't used to. I was glad they'd picked a four-player game, though; it gave me the perfect excuse to get out for a little fresh air. Mostly I wanted to see what Connor might be doing.

We'd had some conversations since the day he arrived, but in the evenings Connor mostly kept to himself. I couldn't really figure it out. He wasn't unfriendly, exactly, but he always seemed to have something on his mind. When I crawled out of the little tent Sue and I shared, I had to walk a little distance in the direction of the dig before I found him. Light spilling from the camp dimly illuminated his form. As Bo had said, he was sitting at the edge of a cliff over the canyon, his scruffy legs crossed in a lotus position as he gazed out at the star-speckled horizon. A full moon was slowly gliding up over the landscape of rock and sand before us. A book sat open in his lap, and his iPod lay in the crease; the flashlight he'd been using to read had also rolled into the book's middle, spilling a column of light out across the canyon and into space. I took a peek at the book's open pages. Egyptian ruins. Didn't we already see those all day?

I wasn't willing to come much closer to the cliff's edge. Although the drop to the winding path below couldn't have been more than twenty feet down, it was nineteen feet farther than I cared to consider falling. Every time I contemplated even low heights, my stomach started to clench and my bowels warned me I'd better not stray too far from the latrine pit.

"What're you listening to?" I asked from a safe distance, crossing my arms to keep the night air from chilling me. When he jerked his head around in surprise, I made some motions of apology. "Sorry."

"Oh, no, it's cool," he said, plucking the buds from his ears. "Just some Yazbek, Stewart Francke, stuff like that."

"Isn't that the Ramesseum?" I nodded at the book in his lap. "I recognized the photos."

"Yeah," he said, blessing me with a smile. "You know it?"

What was it with guys and baseball caps? Connor seemed to have a perfectly lush head of brown hair that curled out from underneath its backward-turned visor, but I'd never seen him remove the thing. The later in the day and the sweatier his hair, the curlier it got. The fuzz on his chin, though, was not something he'd worn the day he arrived. "That's one of the big temples we're supposed to visit at the end of the month, right before we go home. The Ramesseum, Abydos, Deir el Bahri . . ." Hadn't he heard about the field trips? My information seemed to get him really excited. "Hey," I suggested. "It's not that late yet, and the gang's still playing cards in my tent. Want to take a walk?"

He thought it over for a minute, then nodded and leaped to his feet to toss the book into his tent, two beyond my own.

"And what is that hanging from your face, caterpillars?" I asked once we'd started walking. Somehow it just seemed natural to take the path down to the excavation. I mean, we only walked along it, like, three hundred billion times a day.

For a surprised moment he wiped his cheeks. "Oh. It's

just not that easy to shave out here," he admitted, luckily taking my words as the joke I'd intended. "I guess you haven't seen me up close much this week. You've spent a lot of time down in the burial chamber with Dr. Battista."

Did he sound jealous? I thought he might, but I didn't have the courage to ask. I let us walk on for a while before replying. "Yeah, well, there's not much to look at down there," I told him. "Rubble. Lots of rubble." And mummies. And darkness. And no air. And the sense of doom that at any minute that one little burial shaft was going to close over my head and trap me fifty feet below the earth to turn into a mummy myself. Ever since I'd gone down there to deliver that stupid tube of documents, I'd been the one kid from the excavation team allowed in the chamber to start sifting through the head-high dense columns of rubble. "And, you know, I get to kind of dab away at it with a big old makeup brush, and if I'm really good, sometimes I get to use my trowel."

I'd never before seen the moon so bright. Maybe I'd just never really been away from the city, where nature always seemed like an afterthought beyond the big buildings and the streetlights and the neon. Here it felt more . . . I don't know. Elemental. "That sounds incredible," Connor said.

I'd pulled out a tube of marionberry-flavored lip gloss. The dry air of the Egyptian desert did a fantastic job of preserving ancient artifacts, but it chapped like you would not believe. My trusty gloss kept my lips moist, and the smell reminded me of home. "Incredibly *dull*," I laughed, trying to make a joke while I applied the stuff.

Apparently it was the wrong thing to say. "You're kidding. I'd *kill* to work down there."

"Yeah, well, it's not bad," I said, swaggering a little. I could hear the envy so plainly in his voice that I could've plucked it up and molded it like green Play-Doh. "And Anca's pretty cool."

"You call Dr. Battista by her first name?"

In my head I surely did, but never, ever would I dare call her anything but Dr. Battista to her face. That would be something like walking up to the pope and giving him a high five, winking, and saying, *Yo, your holy-butt dy-no-mighty.* Utterly unthinkable, in other words. "You know how it is when you work closely with someone," I told him, leaving out the part about how Dr. Battista and her crew worked on the opposite end of the burial chamber from little old me and my sifted grit and grime. Every hour I'd carry the full rubber baskets to the hook hanging down the burial shaft so they could be lifted to the surface. "You get kind of tight."

"What's she like?"

When I looked over my shoulder, the camp was a comfortable cluster of lights at the top of the canyon. The air grew cooler the farther we strolled. I heard occasional voices from below. They comforted the squirming 'fraidy-cat in me. "Really brilliant," I said, not at all untruthfully this time. "No nonsense. Smart. She's not afraid of anything."

"So," he drawled, shuffling along beside me. The beam from his flashlight danced along on the ground in front of us. "Kind of like you, then."

The flush flew to my cheeks before I could stop it. Thank goodness that in the moonlight we both looked pale. "I'm not," I said, surprised at how husky my voice sounded. I cleared my throat and choked down the emotion. "Really, I'm not."

"Aw, come on, everyone knows you're the leader on our team," he said. "You go places other people won't, you climb up and down ladders like they're nothing. You've obviously got the smarts or you wouldn't even be here, right? I mean, the first glance I got of you was laying the smack-down on an Egyptian scorpion, for Pete's sake. Even at home you run with the popular crowd."

"Nah," I said, trying to sound casual. Inwardly, though, the Queen of Denial was aching to get out. *I'm scared!* she wanted to say. *I'm a fake! None of what you see is real! I'm not smart! I didn't even write an essay!* I cleared my throat again to give myself time to calm down. "You're the one here on scholarship, after all."

"Exsqueeze me? You too!" he countered. "And I thought I was modest."

Oh, God. Was I on scholarship? Seriously? How could I not have a clue? You know, considering how I spent most of the month before the trip hiding under my bed (meta-phorically speaking, anyway . . . in reality I'd stayed *in* bed with the covers pulled up over my head), my parents could have mentioned scholarships a hundred times and I would have missed it because I was thinking about all the scary things that were going to happen to me. I wanted to change the subject. "So how's rooming with Bo?" I asked him as we rounded the path at the bottom of the hill. In the quiet, my voice sounded unnaturally loud.

"Bo's a cool guy. It's living next to Rona McDonald that's a pain in the butt," he said. He sounded slightly ashamed to be calling Dag by her nickname. "On and on and on . . . that woman talks just to hear her own voice, I swear to God."

I felt more comfortable again. When we weren't dis-cussing me—or the fake me, or the me who wasn't me—I felt good talking to Connor. It almost made me wish I'd known him more back in Seattle. How in the world could a girl like me be real friends with someone like Connor,

47

though? He might not have run with Baz Wilder's gang, but he surely never lacked for company. "Have you heard her go on about curses of the mummy's tomb?"

"Oh, man!" He laughed. "Amazing!"

"I don't know why they have someone on a dig who keeps filling kids' minds with stupid stuff about curses."

"I know!" he said. "I mean, jeez, everyone knows they don't exist."

Whew. My heart thumped a little, relieved. Yeah, I knew they didn't exist, but somehow it made it a little more believable to hear someone else say it aloud. What I didn't expect was to hear a deep voice in the darkness repeat it.

"Dagmar Sorensson is highly superstitious. There is no such thing as a curse."

The beam from Connor's flashlight bounced around the steep rock walls until at last it bobbed over a handsome, dark-skinned face. I nearly screamed and jumped out of my skin. I'd thought we were alone. "Seth!" I felt like someone had reached down into my gullet and yanked the word out of me. "It is Seth, right?"

His white teeth seemed to rival the moon in brilliance. "Yes. It is I."

"What are you doing out here?" I asked him. Mentally, I added, *And looking so hot in those tight jeans and that leather jacket?*

"I was taking a walk," he said, with an unexpected cheeky grin. It made me think there was more to his words. "Excuse me," he said, looking at Connor. "WXYZ."

Connor seemed confused for a minute. "Huh?"

Seth raised his eyebrows, and with patience repeated, "W. X. Y. Z. I believe that is the expression?"

I, unfortunately, knew exactly what Seth was trying to tell

48

him. Three brothers, remember? You run into it a lot. I cleared my throat. "It's just XYZ. Your pants?" I said to Connor. "They're a little bit unzipped. And when I say a little, I mean totally."

Connor let loose with an annoyed swear word and turned around to take care of matters. In his place I would have been utterly mortified, but maybe when you're a boy, an open fly doesn't really amount to much.

"I was walking up to camp to find you, anyway. I was hoping we could have a little . . . talk," Seth said.

"Oh? What about?" In the pool of glowing moonlight, Connor turned back around and smoothed down his shorts. Seth just flexed his arms so that his ropy muscles jumped in time with my thumping heart. Man, was he ever tasty. In answer to my question, he raised his eyebrows. Obviously Seth didn't want to talk about something in front of Connor. But what . . . ?

Oh. He wanted to talk about *that*. "I see," I said.

"Hey, I'd better get back up to camp." Connor somehow seemed to realize that Seth wanted alone time with me. It was only then that I remembered Connor had been present a few days before to catch Seth and me in that embarrassing kiss on top of the ladder. The memory made me blush once again. I stepped back from Seth and drew closer to Connor.

"You don't have to go," I told him.

Connor looked from me to Seth, and then back at me again. "Um, yeah. I think I do." Seth just looked at the stars in the sky and cracked his knuckles, one by one. It sounded like popcorn time at the local movie house. Over the jarring noise, Connor held out his hand. "You should take the flashlight."

"Oh, no, you—"

His fingertips closed over mine as he pressed the heavy torch into my hand. "You take it," he repeated. "I don't want anything happening to you." With a curt nod at Seth, he turned and left us.

Four

Connor scuffled his way back up the stone and gravel of the path, leaving me to blink after him. I felt strangely touched. He didn't want anything happening to me? Really?

Seth spoke up. "Strange kid, who cannot spare a moment to keep his pants closed."

It was just an offhand comment, but for some reason it really irritated me. "You know, we get up at six in the morning, eat and have study session until ten, then work for seven hours stooped over in the dust with breaks only for lunch and dinner. By the time it gets around to this time of night and we change into clean clothes that aren't much cleaner than our filthy clothes, we're pretty much walking zombies," I informed him. "It's a wonder we're not all stumbling around with our zippers down. And he's not a kid. He's only a year younger than you." I blinked at myself. Frightened Chloe would never have made a speech like that. She would have just nodded at Seth, chuckled a little, and felt guilty for days after.

"You have a temper!" Seth laughed. "I meant no offense." He must have noticed how I shivered, because in one fluid and muscular motion he shuffled his arms from his black leather jacket. He wrapped it around my shoulders, once again enveloping me in that musky, cologned smell I associated with him. Instantly I felt a little warmer. "So . . ." he said, as if searching for words.

"What's all this about?" I asked him. Half of me was scared to hear the answer.

"Well." He laughed and lifted his hands above his head. In the moonlight his tight T-shirt clung to every curve of his chest. "The other day, when we, well—"

"Kissed?" I finished for him.

He grinned at his own version. "I was going to say, if I've learned the expression correctly, when you macked down on me."

"Macked down! In your dreams!" I countered. "And that's the *only* place you'll be getting any of that from me again."

"That's what I wanted to talk about," he said, plunging his hands into his jeans pockets. "You knew the kiss was nothing serious, am I right?"

"Sure," I replied, even before I thought about it. I hadn't thought about that kiss since it happened, really. I'd not walked away from it thinking there'd be more. It had been an experiment. Something I tried just to see if I could. Yeah, he was hotness personified, but I hope I'm not so desperate that I have to put the flirt on every guy who's easy to look at. "Oh, yeah, totally. I mean, you and me? Not." I laughed lightly to show him there weren't any hard feelings.

He looked a little put out at that. "What do you mean? Do you think there's something wrong with me?" Was he back on the gay thing again? Honestly, guys are way too hung up on that.

"No, not at all. It's just ridiculous, that's all."

His thick eyebrows crunched together. "I don't think I'm that ridiculous."

The conversation was getting surreal. Here was half of the most gorgeous slabs of twin hotness I'd ever known, trying to break up a relationship that never existed, and I was having to reassure *his* ego. Why couldn't any of this kind of experience translate into high school credit? "Listen," I told him patiently, moving a little closer. I hugged the jacket to my shoulders. "It was just one of those moments. Blame it on the monkeys if you have to. But I didn't think it was anything more than what it was—it was only a quick smooch. Right?" He nodded. "So we're friends, right?"

"Yes," he said. "Friends."

I put my hands on his shoulders, stood on tiptoe, and gave him a kiss on the lips. Nothing major. Nothing with tongue. Just a friendly kiss. The flashlight's beam danced over our faces as it happened. "And that's that," I said, before moving away again.

"Well, you were easier to deal with than I thought."

Now it was my turn for the eyebrow crunch. "I don't think I'm *that* much of a basket case."

He laughed. "Nothing like that. Now, as a consolation prize you may show me around Tekhen and Tekhnet's burial chamber."

"Some prize!" It took a moment of his expectant waiting for me to realize he was serious. "Wait a minute. You're not kidding? You know it's locked this time of night!"

"I'm the son of the excavation's director," he said. "You think they'll refuse me?"

I hadn't thought of that. I clenched up at the thought, though. The burial chamber, alone, after dark? The heck! "So go on in yourself! You know where stuff is."

"Yes, but"—his voice was smooth and sweet, like Egyptian honey—"you're the one who can give me the guided tour, right?" He had to be crazy. There was no way! "Do not tell me that of all people, you are scared."

He had only been joking, of course. Yet when you're like me and spend every waking minute of every day convincing yourself and everyone else that you're unflappable, you react to jokes like his with anger. I tried to keep it hidden, but only barely managed. "I'm not scared of anything," I spat at him. "You want to go?"

"Yes, I want to go," he retorted, matching my toughness.

"So let's go!" I shouted.

"I'm going!"

What was I doing? Even my made-up persona didn't want to break the rules. If there was anything consistent between the Queen of Denial and her sassy alter ego, it was that I never, never, *never* did anything to get into trouble with teachers and parents and officials. And this was definitely going to be trouble, I could tell right from the start. Once we were at the bottom of the canyon at the west entrance to the Tombs of the Servitors, Seth barked at the night guards in rapid-fire Arabic. I couldn't really tell what they were saying, but the tone sounded hostile. It sounded like they were arguing, actually. "*Ma fish Kahraba!*" Seth yelled at one point. "*Ma fish Kahraba!*" He pointed to one guard's head.

The guard looked annoyed. With obvious reluctance he finally tossed a small ring of keys in Seth's direction. He didn't speak again until we were walking away and our backs were turned. It sounded derogatory.

Seth whirled. "*Inta khaywan!*" he snarled. The two guards' mutters quickly vanished.

By that point instinct was telling me to turn tail and head

back to camp. Between the prospect of visiting the tomb in the dark, the unwelcoming guards, and the sheer weirdness of it all, I didn't want any part of this mess. "What was that all about?" I asked him.

"They are pigs," he said. "Just forget it."

I let it go. I had too much else on my mind. I knew what happened in Egyptian tombs at night. I saw that guy get his faced sucked dry in *The Mummy.*

No, that was just the Queen of Denial, sticking her head out of her little closet. I firmly closed the door and wedged it tightly shut. *The Mummy* was just a movie. *And let's get real,* I told myself. How in the world was I going to tell the difference between the tomb at night and the tomb during the day? It's not like the burial chamber had bay windows with a pretty view outside. Dark was dark, no matter on what side of the earth the sun happened to be.

Inside me, though, I kept hearing a small voice: *But . . . But . . . !*

My oldest brother, Walter, once had a hamster who was absolutely, totally afraid of everyone except him. Whenever Ryan or Jesse or I would come into the room, the poor little thing would freeze, run, freeze, and realize there was nowhere to run to in his little plastic cage, try to run, find another wall, then freeze and run again. Eventually it would just fly around the cage in circles, so scared that it couldn't even think, making noises and scattering litter until finally Walter would ask us *please* to stop bothering his hamster or he'd break our necks.

I'd spent way too much of my life being that small, scared animal. I wasn't a hamster. I was a sixteen-year-old girl. I was practically an adult. Year after next I might be going off to college—with all the time I'd spent on extracurriculars for the sake of my college résumé, believe you me, college had *better* be worth it.

So while Seth fumbled with the keys to the iron grille over the entrance to the tomb, I tried to calm myself down. I'd spent six or more hours a day for the last week beyond that gaping hole in the rock. I'd been up and down the rope ladder so many times that lately I didn't even need to give myself the usual pep talk. Even the mummies . . . Well, I kept away from the mummies. It's like someone else's barking dog. You might believe it's not going to bite you, but you still don't rub steak over your fingers, hold out your hand, and take your chances.

"That's funny," he said, when I'd managed to calm down my breathing from an asthmatic wheeze to a soft rasp. The grille swung open. "It wasn't locked."

Ever since the time when Egyptian kings had the bright idea of interring the bodies of the royals and their highest servants into rock caverns chipped from desert stone, people have been looking to plunder the tombs for their gold and artifacts. It's a shame that mankind's not changed very much in four thousand years. Without the guards and the locks, there'd be very little left for archaeologists to look at or to study. Tourists and thieves could chip away at the sculptures and plaster for little souvenirs or pieces to sell on the black market. It's no wonder that the last words any archaeologist wants to hear are *treasure* or *gold*, because all it does is bring out bandits who want to make a profit for themselves. While Tekhen and Tekhnet weren't exactly King Tut, there might be a lot of people out there who'd like little pieces of the manicurists to the queen. Renegade tourists from a beauty school from Biloxi, maybe.

"Those guards will be in serious trouble when my father hears of this." Seth paused for a second, swinging the door back and forth. "Maybe this was a bad idea. I should get you back to camp."

It's weird how the notion of someone else getting into trouble calms you down, isn't it? "Now who's weak-kneed?" I asked him. "Are we going in, or am I going to have to tell everyone you're all bark and no bite?"

"You are quite cheeky for a girl wearing someone's borrowed bomber jacket," he said, shaking his head. "All right. Let's do it."

"About time!"

I had been wrong about one thing: The tomb was a lot different at night. For one thing, during the daytime we had the generator running for the lights—and right now that would attract attention. When we tripped down the stairs (literally) and into the antechamber, the flashlight's beam barely illuminated the half-cleaned walls. It was so dark that if we'd walked back outside, the moonlight would have been blinding. "Okay," Seth admitted. "This is quite spooky."

"Ssssh!" I held a finger to my lips and shone the flashlight on my face from under my chin to make it look eerie. "Listen!"

"What?" Seth's voice dropped to a whisper. I thought I heard a little panic in it.

"It's the curse of the mummies!" I intoned, breaking out into a giggle.

"Chloe," he said, "you are one mean girl."

"You were scared!"

"I was not," he grumped. "I can't believe you."

He grabbed the flashlight then and stomped off ahead of me. I was so surprised at his desertion that it took me a moment to catch on. Strange, though: Right before I bolted after him, I thought I heard a noise. Something like shuffling, something like breathing. Maybe a combination of both. It made me hold my breath and draw the collar of Seth's jacket tightly around my neck.

Maybe I was just scaring myself, though. I'd spent a lifetime scaring myself.

"Thanks for waiting," I complained when I caught up halfway down the slanted stairway. He still looked annoyed, probably that I'd spooked him a little.

"Don't you hear enough of that mummy nonsense from Dag day in and day out?" He sounded sulky still.

It felt good to have the upper hand here. He was probably more frightened than I. When we reached the shaft, I kicked at the rope ladder with my toe. "You first or me?" When he hesitated, I decided to show off. "Me then."

I plopped down onto the rock and swung my legs over the edge so expertly, it seemed as if I'd been doing it for years. "It's not that hard." The flashlight blinded me for a moment as he shone it down the shaft. "Even for a boy."

"Funny," he said, without a trace of humor. "Just hurry up."

Locating the floor was a little more difficult without electricity. I half worried that I'd bang my kneecaps against the bedrock. Luckily I'd memorized all twenty-seven rungs of the ladder on my many panicked trips down. "Coming?" I called. My voice sounded incredibly loud in the low-ceilinged chamber.

"All right, all right," I heard him mumble.

"It's not far," I encouraged, as I heard him mutter to himself. Showers of dust fell down onto my face, making me cough and rub my eyes and back away. "Bleah!"

"The ladder's shaking," he said. His legs appeared below the ceiling as his feet groped for a grip.

"Aw, come on, Little Miss Muffet, get your tuffet down here already," I jeered up at him. "What the . . . !"

I leaped back as the flashlight plummeted to the ground with a terrible thudding sound. It landed on its plastic handle, bounced back into the air, and arced in the direction of a yard-high pile of loose rubble—one of the many that I'd not yet gotten to with my sieve and my trowel. It landed just short of the pile. I heard the sound of plastic popping and something else clattering on the rock. Everything went dark.

I know it's silly, but in the absolute darkness everything seemed thirty degrees colder. I wouldn't give in to fear, though. I channeled it into anger. "You could have killed me!" I complained. I'd been standing in that spot only moments before. Good thing I'd moved out of the way!

"I don't know what happened," I heard him say. He sounded genuinely shaken.

"Just stay still."

Okay. I'd seen where the flashlight landed. If I groped my way over to the rubble very carefully . . . I felt my shoe collide with something that started to roll away, so I dropped to a squat and scrabbled on the floor until my fingers touched something heavy and cylindrical, with a nub at one end. A battery. I groped around some more and felt my fingertips brush against the gritty dust of the rubble pile. I rubbed them raw on the rough surface of the bedrock until at last I stumbled on something smooth and familiar. The flashlight case! And the other battery somehow had managed not to be ejected from its inside.

I plopped in the cell I'd already found. That's when I realized I needed to find the flashlight's snap-on base, or else the lamp's current couldn't flow. "Hold on!" I shouted. It had to be around there someplace. No need to panic, right?

"I can't find a foothold," I heard Seth say above. I could hear the rope ladder rustling on the floor behind me.

"Just hang tight a minute."

I groped around the rubble to see if the plastic end might have bounced here. Somehow I unlodged something, and a minor avalanche of small rocks and dirt cascaded onto the back of my hand. Damn it! I wedged the flashlight between my thighs and started to scrape around in the debris in case my accident had covered it up.

"Got it!" I cried as my fingers curled around something round. But no—I'd found something else. Whatever was in my hand was like an oversize ring or a bucket handle, definitely too big to fit inside a flashlight. This was more like a door knocker. Maybe it attached to the outside. Or had Seth dropped something else? I stuck the object in a jacket pocket and fumbled around some more until, on the bare bedrock a few inches away from the edge of the pile, I finally found the little plastic cap. Hallelujah!

I was screwing it back on when disaster struck. Seth gave a hoarse yell. I felt a swoosh of air, and then with a rush of noise and yelling, he crashed to the rock floor. I held my breath. Was he dead? After a moment I heard a mixed stream of Arabic and English. I'd never been so relieved to hear swearing in my entire life.

The flashlight's beam was wobbly and weak when I flipped it back on, but within a moment it flickered back to normal. "Seth!" I swore, running to his side. He lay in the pool of light, face screwed up in pain. "Are you okay? Are you hurt? Are you broken? Where does it hurt? What happened? Are you hurt?"

"Just . . . shut . . . up!" he growled at me, trying to sit up.

"Don't move!" He didn't listen to me. I scrabbled down beside him and looked for bones protruding where they shouldn't. His hand was still pressed to his forehead. "Let me see." When I pried away the heel of his hand from his brow, it came away sticky and red. "You're bleeding. I don't know what to do about bleeding. My parents made me take CPR for my college résumé. Do you need CPR?" I babbled.

"I know I'm bleeding! And I don't need bloody CPR!"

"You need a doctor."

"You think?" He let out a wheeze of pain.

"Don't move," I repeated. I laid the flashlight on the floor so he'd have light, stood up, and rushed to our only escape out. Something was wrong with the rope ladder, though. It hung at an odd angle, its rungs slack and crooked, as if it had been twisted around and around. Could I climb it?

Did I even have a choice?

"Keep some pressure on that bleeding," I told him, stalling. Somewhere in the back of my head, probably from playing the victim when my brothers were training for their Boy Scout first aid badges, I remembered that even a minor head wound could cause someone to bleed like crazy. Still, I didn't want him to take chances. What if he lost quarts of the stuff before I could get up the ladder and come back with some help? What if he passed out? What if he died? I'd have his blood on my hands. Literally!

All the more reason to get up that ladder then, I told myself.

I lifted up my right foot and wedged it into the tangle of rope, then raised myself up. "I'll be right back," I told him. "Don't be scared."

I was crazy. I was absolutely, totally, utterly bonkers-crazy, climbing a mess of rope when I knew I could also end up on the floor beside Seth with my head bashed in. Or worse. I didn't have an option, though. No one would come looking for us. No one would know we were here except the guards, and Seth hadn't exactly been friendly to them. Hand over hand I hauled myself up, catching wobbling footholds in the corners of each rung. I was crazy. Absolutely insane.

I could sense I was near the top by the sound of my breathing, which began to echo in the chamber above. Thank God. I was nearly there.

Without warning I was blinded by light. Someone's flashlight burned holes in my retinas. For a panicked second I thought I was going to lose my grip on my ladder. I clutched the rope until its spiky fibers made my eyes water, and knew I would be okay. "Chloe?" someone asked above me. "Don't move."

"Who's that?" I asked. There was something about the voice I recognized. "Connor?" I asked, pulling myself up another rung.

"Don't . . . seriously, don't . . ."

I felt his hand grab my upper arm as I clawed for the surface. "The heck! What are you doing?" I was utterly surprised when he started to haul me up with such force that I knew I'd have enormous hand-shaped bruises on the undersides of my biceps tomorrow. He wasn't graceful about it, either. Next thing I knew, we were a tangle of arms and legs and torsos on the side of the shaft's opening. "What is the BFD?" I asked him, seriously annoyed at his intervention.

He didn't have to say a word. He just aimed the beam of his flashlight at the floor stakes supporting the ladder.

One of them was intact and perfectly fine.

The other one was missing.

Five

Zzzzzhnnnnuknunk!

I tossed on my cot and screwed my eyes shut tight.

Mmmm-mmm-mmm-shmack-shmack-shmack.

My fate was sealed. I was never going to sleep, ever again.

Zzzzzhnnnnuknunk! That did it. My eyelids both felt as if they'd been stapled shut, painted with superglue, and sealed with concrete, but I managed to wrench open one of them so I could stare at Dagmar Sorensson, asleep and snoring on her cot. Since I could clearly see her splotchy, red-freckled face and the curlers in her hair, and even observe her nose twitch with every snore, it had to be dawn. Once again she drew in breath with her mighty Nordic lungs, and blew it out through her lips and nose.

Mmmm-mmm-mmm-shmack-shmack-shmack. Kathy Klemper's cot occupied the other side of the tent from Dag. As if answering the chaperone's nasal howl, she shifted in her sleep and smacked her lips. Not a quiet, content smacking. Her lips and tongue came together in a gulping wet sucking sound that I likened to the kind of noise an uncouth cannibal might make while slurping the marrow out of his victims' bones after he'd made a tasty supper on the flesh, before a big belch.

I wanted to murder them both. Instead I pulled the pillow over my head and wished for the third morning in a row that I were dead.

By the evening I was in even worse shape. It felt like the world had taken a mallet to me and played croquet with my head for an entire day. Sue peered at me with concern. "Sleeping badly still?" she asked me as the cook slopped some green stuff on top of the gray stuff that was lying next to the toasted brown stuff. I wasn't sure I even wanted to figure out what any of it was.

"Does it show?" I grabbed a bottle of root beer from the table, then took a couple more for my backpack.

"A little. Under the eyes. On a scale of one to ten, where one is perky and ten is the living dead, I'd say about a six." We put our trays on the table and sat between the other kids on the excavation team. "*Elle c'est* sex," she said to Mallorie.

"Sex?" repeated the French girl, choking on her cream soda.

"Sex?" asked Bo, not bothering to wipe his lips.

Deidre looked into her pitiful dinner. "I don't even want to know."

"Sex. Sex! Sex!" Sue held up the five fingers of one hand and one on the other.

Mallorie imitated her. "Six?" she questioned.

When the rest of us finished laughing, Sue shrugged. "Any one of you can take over the translation job anytime now. Just let me know."

Connor didn't join us in the big mess tent until we were nearly finished. As usual, he had a book tucked underneath his arm and his iPod on his hip and brown curls swelling from under the sides and back of his baseball cap. He'd cleaned up the scruffiness on his face, though. It still seemed he was trying to grow facial hair of some kind, but at least now it looked a little more like a beard and a little less like leprosy.

He stared at me while balancing his book and tray to set them both onto the table. "You look like total crap. No offense," he added quickly.

"Good evening to you too," I snapped at him, though not with any real anger. "You could have warned me that Dag and the Klemper both snore like Looney Tunes characters."

Speak of the devil—the pair appeared in the door of the mess tent, looking down their noses at the scientists and the servers and the workers and at us alike. Both appeared suspiciously clean. They made me want to grind my teeth. It sounds like a little thing to anyone who hasn't spent two weeks out in the middle of the desert, but consider the way it feels to skip showering for a day. After eleven days, multiply by about a hundred. Water theft wasn't murder in the first degree, but if they were using more than their ration for sponge baths we weren't getting, they were stealing from the rest of us.

"Oh, yeah." Connor grinned, brandishing his earbuds. "You kind of learn to tune out the commotion. Shame you have to deal with it."

That was certainly the truth. It was the biggest shame of the month that the night of the accident, the Dig Egypt! chaperone had moved me—lock, stock, and lip gloss—into the larger tent with her and Kathy Klemper. I was being the bad influence, she had yelled at me. I was being the irresponsible childrens. With her red wedge bobbing and spit-

65

tle flying from her mouth, Dag had informed me in no uncertain terms that I was being the loose large gun that is
shooting the round balls at pirate ships.

I had to think that one over for a minute. "Loose cannon?" I finally asked.

"Yes, you are being the loose cannon and endangerment
to Dig Egypt! We are being guests here among many important pipples and in one night are you ruining many
many months of work!" I had cringed as she leaned in
closer and closer, deadly serious. "You are nearly killing son
of important man and ruining ladder to burial chamber!"

"It did that on its own!" I protested. Inwardly, though, I
remembered the sounds I might have heard of someone
else skulking in the tomb with us and added, *Or was cut.*

Those noises could have been my imagination, but one
thing wasn't: If it hadn't been widely believed that Seth had
taken me to the burial chamber instead of the other way
around, my butt would have been on a plane back to Seattle. "I am thinking of sending you back home! I am chaperone! I can be doing this thing!" Dag had yelled, nearly
making me cry.

Every time I remembered that night, I shivered. Dagmar
had a perfect right to send any of us on either the excavation or conservation teams back home at a moment's notice—it was a threat she used about as often as she pulled
her mouth into a point and sniffed with disgust. Pretty often, in other words. During my first couple of days in Egypt
I would've been fine with being sent home. Part of me even
wished I'd thought of it sooner. After making friends with
Sue and Bo and Deidre, though, and after taking care of
Mallorie, I didn't want to make so quick an exit. I liked
those guys. They looked up to me. They didn't think of me

as a liability or a hanger-on. To them I was a friend—the real thing.

And then there was Connor, who had worried enough about Seth's intentions to fetch another flashlight from camp and evade the guards and follow our trail. How could I not melt at his kind gesture?

"I don't want to go," I had told Dag. "Please don't send me away. Please!"

Dag had flared her nostrils in triumph. She had me just where she wanted me. "Then you are to be staying in big tent under my eyeballs!" she decreed. "And you are not to be sneaking off in middle of night for kissy-kissy with boys!"

"Okay, okay," I'd said. I didn't know how she'd known I'd given Seth a no-hard-feelings kiss that night. Maybe she thought all American girls were reckless Jezebels at heart.

I'd moved my mess into the big tent that night. And that's when my insomnia began.

"I miss you, Clo," Sue told me as she pushed away the remains of her dinner slop. "It's scary in the tent all alone at night." She dug in her over-the-shoulder pack for her little cosmetics bag and pulled from it a lipstick and her mirror. Once she'd freshened her mouth a little, she pulled out an eyeliner and eye-shadow kit and began working on the rest of her face.

"Oh. My. God," said Bo, fascinated by her little performance. "I can't believe you girls and makeup. You even put on the stuff before we go work in the tombs. Who can see you're wearing it?"

"*I* know I'm wearing it," Sue said with a degree of stiffness. She murmured the approximate French translation to Mallorie before replying again. When I'd bunked with Sue,

I'd figured out her parents weren't exactly hurting for money. I suspected that if I ever visited her in L.A. I'd find she was one of those girls with an outfit and an eyebrow brush for every occasion. Not high-maintenance, exactly— out here in the desert, none of us could afford to be high-maintenance. Sue was just sophisticated. "And that's all that matters."

"Dude, you wouldn't catch the slaves building the pyramids worrying about their makeup," Bo countered. "I'm just saying, is all."

I cleared my throat. "Actually there's a lot of evidence that would prove you wrong," I told him. Sue and Mallorie looked over with interest; Bo just gaped. Connor, though, stared at me over the top of his dinner book. It was his attention that most encouraged me to continue. "There are a lot of ancient paintings that show eye makeup being applied to everyone from royals to slaves, including those who worked on the pyramids." Connor had put down his book by now. I had everyone's attention. "The ancient Egyptians were big on makeup. They've found vials and vials in tombs, and when they analyzed it with, like, cyclotrons and stuff, they found out that the Egyptians weren't just slapping ingredients together. They had a whole industry devoted to making the chemicals that went into their cosmetics."

Even Sue had stopped in the middle of her blush application to listen to me.

"Some Egyptian pharaohs even owned their own mines of galena, this shiny black mineral they used. If they ground it up really fine, for over an hour, it came out like matte makeup. If they just pounded it a little bit, it would be all glossy and stuff," I said. "And everyone wore it. Men and women. Rich people and slaves. Those guys on the pyramid? It was doubly important they put on their makeup every morning. Some of the minerals in their eyeliners had, like, chemicals that kept bacteria and flies away from their face while they worked; plus the dark color absorbed glare from the sun. You know, kind of like how football players put those black marks on their cheekbones when they suit up for a game. There's actually a lot of hieroglyphics that talk about the recipes the Eyptians used for their cosmetics."

Everyone at the table was quiet when I finished. "Oh. My. God," said Bo for the second time that morning. He looked glum. "First mummy manicurists. Then makeup tips in hieroglyphics. I am so going home from this a total *girl*."

Our combined laughter was loud enough that some of the multilingual chatter at the other tables died down as heads turned to look at us. "You're too hung up on this manicurist thing," Connor told him. I hadn't seen Connor in good spirits much; he was such a serious guy that the sudden appearance of a smile made it seem like a holiday. "It was just a job. An important job."

I nodded at Connor. "The Egyptians were really caught up in the way they looked. They weren't that different from us, like that. They were totally into their hair and makeup and skin and clothes and, yeah, even their nails. When they excavated King Tutankhamen, they found his mummy wrapped with jewelry all over his body and little gold tips on his fingers that were supposed to give him a permanent manicure in his afterlife with the gods."

"It's *so* unfair that you're supersmart, too, with everything else going for you," Deidre complained, covering her plate with her paper napkin and shoving it away.

"I'm not smart!" It seemed a weird thing to be arguing about.

"Chloe, smart?" Kathy Klemper appeared at the empty seat at the head of the table. "What person in a coma are you comparing her to?" She put her dinner tray on our table and sat down. Simultaneously the five of us pushed back our benches and stood up. Even Mallorie, who always looked at Kathy as if she were a bad Camembert.

Our desertion upset Kathy. She grabbed my wrist and stood back up when without a word I followed the others to the waste bins. "You'd better not be running off on your own again tonight," she said in a low voice. "I'd really hate for Dag to find out and send you home."

I wanted to wipe that sneer right off her face. "You know what, Kathy?" I asked her. She raised her eyebrows in response. "You smell like soap."

That settled it. She plopped down into her seat with a slightly guilty expression and involved herself with her dehydrated chipped beef. Dag was across the room, pointing her finger at a pair of junior archaeologists, neither of whom looked any too thrilled to wrap their brains around her loopy Swedish-tinged lecture. I could tell Dag had her eye on me, though, and if I didn't skedaddle my butt out of there, I'd be next. "Let's go," I murmured to Connor. "I want to drop off these root beers in my tent."

Outside in the last of the day's hazy sunshine, sand-covered hills and valleys dipped and rose in the direction of Luxor and the Nile. "I have to put my book away too," he told me. Even though the others were only about ten steps ahead of us, I liked walking behind with Connor. Ever since the night he'd pulled me up from the burial shaft, we'd had this special thing between us.

I can see my English teacher back home circling that word, *thing,* and writing in red ink the letter V for *vague.* But what could I call it? Romance? Mmmmm, I don't know.

Rapport? Maybe. It felt like we were supposed to hang around together on this trip. We were the only kids from the same school. If you didn't count Kathy Klemper—and who wanted to?—we were the only kids in Dig Egypt! from the same city. It felt like we should be friends.

"Boy, you really know your stuff." He dug his hands deep into the pockets of his painter's pants and clutched his book under his armpit. "That was pretty impressive back there."

"Oh. That." I tried to keep my tone offhand and light. "That was nothing." Did I sound arrogant? I worried I sounded like one of those stupid know-it-alls everyone more or less despises whenever they open their mouths. What did genuinely smart people do when they got compliments like that? They were probably gracious. They probably quoted Shakespeare. I was such a fake.

"No, honestly," he said. "You really know your stuff. No wonder Dr. Battista has made you her right-hand man. Woman. You know what I mean."

That made me laugh. "Hardly!" We shuffled along back in the direction of our tents, passing the guarded trailer where all the important finds from the dig were kept. "Come on, I just picked that up from a special on the National Geographic Channel I watched one time." I glanced over to see how he took the news. He didn't wrinkle his nose, though, or scrunch his lips together in a way that said, *Television! Ew!*

Instead he nodded. "Cool." That was it? A nod? Or was he unsurprised because he had seen through me a long time ago? "Hold a sec," Connor told me, holding out his hands so that I collided with one of them. He quickly removed it before my confused mind could take in the fact that he'd just had a near-breast encounter. "Isn't it incredible?"

"What?" I couldn't figure out what in the world he

71

meant. I saw dirt and dust and sand and drooping canvas tents. I heard the screech of the water tank as someone tried to draw from it water that wasn't there. From the west, a putrid wind o' stench blew from the latrines, and the wild dogs that roamed the camp had left little brown gifties all over the place that only enhanced the smell. "Isn't what incredible?" I asked with a sudden wave of homesickness. "It's okay, but I'd rather be somewhere clean and where everything didn't smell like poop."

"No, this." He swept out his hands again, careful not to grab me in a place he shouldn't. He indicated the broad sweep of the landscape beyond the last of the tents. "All of it. Look at how beautiful the hills are! They're so many shades of red and brown and tan, especially this time of day. I've wanted to be in Egypt for so long. You can't imagine. And now that I'm here . . . it's better than any photograph in any book!" His enthusiasm was so genuine that I couldn't help but begin to see the scenery as he saw it. "Sometimes I come out from the tomb so I can see how the land looks at different times of the day. The shadows crawl up the hills from the west over the morning; then they spill down the sides as the sun sets. Haven't you seen it? You should look, if you can get out of the burial chamber." As his hands gestured, what I'd seen as dull and lifeless cliffs and hills took on a new aspect. They didn't change in appearance, exactly, but where Connor's fingers moved, they seemed to leave behind a trail of . . . what? It was as if he'd taken an old painting I was so used to that I didn't even notice it anymore, and given it one of those classy gold frames you see in museums. The picture I'd ignored day after day turned into something I *wanted* to look at. "And you know that beyond what we can see, the land turns lush and green and fertile where the river flows. Egypt is the cradle of civilization! It's just so amazing! That night we had the full moon . . . it was so beautiful that I didn't want to leave the cliff."

And yet he had left it, I realized. He'd left it for me.

While the other kids walked on to their tents to drop off their soda bottles and snacks, Connor and I stood there at the edge of the Dig Egypt! encampment and stared out at the vista. Or to be entirely accurate, Connor basked in the view. My attention was divided between looking at the landscape and watching Connor. My brain wanted to complain about him the same way Deidre had about me earlier—he was nice, smart, and friendly. It wasn't fair that he was, like, totally fine and visionary, too. I felt a stab of jealousy. "You look like you're drinking it in for the final time," I joked.

His head turned sharply, as if I'd said the very last thing he'd expected. "What do you mean by that?"

I was so taken aback by the snappish tone of his voice that I tried to make light. "I mean, jeez, I know Dag keeps telling us she can send us home anytime she wants, but you don't think she really would, do you? I mean, look at me. I banged up the project director's son and I'm still here." Sleepless and not really on speaking terms with Seth anymore, but yeah, I was still there. I grinned. "Unless you've got some big secret you're hiding." When he didn't answer, I teased some more. "That must be it. You have some big secret and you're worried you're going to be caught."

I'd expected a denial or at least a laugh out of him. I didn't expect the deadly coldness. "Whatever," he said, turning away from me.

I hate that word! Whenever someone flings it in my face I know it means, *You've ticked me off and I really don't think you're worth the effort.* I couldn't believe I was hearing it from Connor's mouth. "Excuse me?" I asked his back as he strode off to his tent. "That was rude!" He walked away, shoulders rigid and stiff and arms clutching his book to his chest. As tough as he was trying to be, he struck me then as brittle and breakable, like fragile glass. One touch might topple him into pieces. "I was joking!" I yelled. He pulled open the front of his tent and disappeared inside.

The heck! What in the world had I said to bring on that kind of reaction?

Maybe I'd touched a nerve because he *had* done something wrong. Connor, though? What in the world could Connor Marsh have done? Don't get me wrong; it's not as if Connor were a straitlaced little prissy pants, but ever since he'd arrived a few days after the rest of us, it was obvious that he was born to be here. He wasn't goofing off and playing dice with the local workers, like Bo sometimes did, or taking extra breaks to brush his hair and apply makeup, like Sue and Mallorie. And he certainly wasn't cowering behind a pile of centuries of flood rubble, peeking out at Dr. Battista as she made her notes and photographs of manicurist mummies, praying for the month to be over, like me. Connor *wanted* to be here. He would never do anything wrong that might put him at risk of getting sent away.

Then again, maybe I wasn't the best judge of what came out of my mouth. If I could get a good night's sleep, I might be able to decode the completely offensive thing I'd just said. It had to be something. Somehow I had to be in the wrong.

It was with a heavy heart that I finally grabbed the rope to the big tent flap and ducked in. If I'd been at home, I would've flung myself onto the bed and spent the rest of the day moping with a book. I didn't have that luxury here.

I didn't have a bed, either, just a cot. And I couldn't fling myself onto that, because someone was sitting on it.

I was so flustered that it took me a minute to put a name to the face of the girl with the curly red hair. "Jan?" I finally asked. What in the world was January James of the conservation team doing in my tent? Was she lost? "Hi . . . what's up?"

Jan tugged at her neckline. I recognized the gesture. I used to do it a lot myself, when my breasts first started making a real appearance and I didn't quite know what to do with them when it felt like everyone was staring at my chest. Even as large as they were, she seemed pretty self-conscious about hers still. Jan even tried to cover them up with a bundle of clothes as she cocked her head and spoke: "Uh."

Somehow I'd expected a little bit more. I blinked. What was this, National Confuse Chloe Day? "Oooookay," I said. "Did you want something?" I dropped the tent flap and started to cross to the back of the tent, where my cot had been wedged in between Dagmar's enormous steamer trunk and a small portable file cabinet she kept locked at all times. I suspected it contained her detailed notes on all the Dig Egypt! kids.

"This is Seth's jacket, isn't it!" Right then I noticed that the bundle of clothes in her lap wasn't hers. They were *mine.* Why in the world was she rooting around in my clothes? Had she been *searching* for Seth's jacket?

"Is it?" I said, trying to be cool. I have to admit, though, that I snatched the jacket from her hands and shook it. She was lucky I didn't fling her out, after the way I found her rummaging around in my stuff. "I guess it is. I should give it back to him."

"It's *his* jacket, not *yours*," she snapped.

I hated the way she lectured me like I was ten and she was the big girl who had to teach me the ways of the world. "Um, I know that, thanks," I told her.

"Did he tell you you could keep it?"

What a snot! "What do you think?" If she had all the answers, why was she even asking? "And what are you even doing here?" Had Seth told her to come get the jacket because he was afraid to face me again? Oooh, he was such a total *boy!*

"Me?" She stammered and hemmed and hawed. "I thought I saw a snake." And the Oscar for Most Unconvincing Excuse in the World to Go Rummaging Through My Stuff goes to . . . January James! "But I guess I didn't. So I'll go. 'Bye." She slid off the cot and stood up.

So Seth wasn't man enough to come get his jacket himself, huh? But why send Jan, of all people, to fetch it for him? It was obvious that in a quick-thinkers race, she and her enormous bosom would be dragging up the rear. If that was the way Seth was going to be, though, maybe he was better off avoiding me, because I sure as hell didn't want to have anything to do with him. "Wait a minute! A snake? Is that the best excuse you can come up with for wanting to go through my things?"

"Ex*cuse* me? Like I want to touch your stuff?"

"What other reason would you have to be sitting on my bed, holding my clothes?"

"I told you, I thought I saw a snake." By now, though, I'd crossed over the border from the Land of Giving a Flying Hoot and into Whatever-ville. I wanted her out of there, so I stared at her and waited for her to go. She only spoke again. "Maybe if your stuff wasn't all over the place, people wouldn't have to touch it to sit down."

"We don't have padded wooden hangers and cold-storage facilities on the excavation team," I said as matter-of-factly as I could. "We're used to doing actual *work* here, not spending our time being pampered at the monastery." I'm not really one for confrontations, but it felt good to let that one fly. And it seemed to leave her speechless, which was a definite check in the plus column. Cold storage, heck. We didn't even have closets out here. I sat down on the cot's other end and ran my hands over the leather.

"What're you doing?"

"Checking the pockets to see if I left anything in them," I told her.

She was about to protest that, I could tell. What did those conservation people think we excavation team kids were, thieves? I was on Dig Egypt! on *scholarship,* thank you very much. I mean, okay, I didn't know that particular fact until I'd been here nearly a week, but my point was just as valid. Before Jan could open her mouth, though, I squinted as someone let in a bright triangle of sunlight. The flap closed again.

It was Connor. "I'm sorry," he said to me, blinking. "I didn't mean to upset you. . . ." His voice trailed off as his eyes adjusted to the dimmer light and he noticed for the first time Jan glaring at him. "Uh."

I searched a couple of the pockets before my hand closed around something round and hard. Oh, yeah. That weird handle part from Connor's flashlight. I hoped he hadn't missed it. I put it behind me and folded the jacket on my lap. "Connor, you know Jan, don't you?"

"Hi," said Connor, crossing his arms at the chest and grabbing his shoulders. "How's it going?"

Anger exploded from her. "Yes, I know *him.* I just hope he knows the *real* you."

"Excuse me?" said Connor and I simultaneously. We looked at each other in surprise. You could have knocked me over with a feather. Where in the world was all that rage coming from? I'd never done a thing to Jan! We'd barely said boo since the first day!

It was time to end this nonsense. "Since you're so hot and bothered about the jacket, you take it." When I held out Seth's duds, January snatched it without thanks. I worked up a silent lather as she shook the jacket out and inspected it—for what? Lipstick stains? Scorpions? A basket of asps? Finally she tossed it over her arm and sniffed.

"*I'm* not the one who's all hot and bothered. You'd better be really, really careful," she told Connor on her way out.

"Whatever!" I called after her as I stood up and moved a few steps after her. I meant it, too. No matter what scarab she or Seth had up their butts, neither of those mutants was worth the weirdness.

Connor, on the other hand, looked agog. "What was *that* all about?"

"I have *no* idea," I assured him. "You know how snotty she and Izumi are. She made it seem like we were living like savages out here."

"We are living like savages out here," Connor pointed out.

"Yeah. Well." We looked at each other then, and laughed. He looked at me shyly. His eyes were the soft Connor eyes I'd learned to enjoy all that week, and not the hard, icy, scary eyes I'd seen a few minutes before.

"I just wanted to say I was sorry. About a few minutes ago. You know." I nodded at the apology. "I was being abnormal. Just a little . . . You know how it is so far away from home."

I felt relief right then. Oh, boy, did I ever know how that was. "Yeah," I said, nodding again.

"So really. I don't want you and me . . . I mean, I think it's cool being around you, and you know, you're so popular you could pick anyone else to hang with, and I don't want to be out of the running, so . . ."

That was just plain embarrassing. "I don't want to hang with anyone else. I mean, I'm not that popular," I amended quickly, so it didn't sound too forward.

"You're sure not popular with Jan," he said, jutting out his lower teeth and widening his eyes while he pretended fright. "She's a little bit scary."

"What a freak! I think she's out to get me for some reason," I said, laughing along. "Anyway. No, everything's cool. Don't worry about it. I like you too." We bobbed our heads. Everything was cool. We bobbed some more. Finally I realized how stupid we looked, bouncing our necks like they were springs and we were special collector's-edition archaeologist bobbleheads on someone's dashboard. "Oh, hey," I told him, heading back to the bed. "When your flashlight broke the other night I accidentally forgot to give you part of it back."

"I don't think so," he said behind me. "It's a little scuffed up, but it works okay."

"Then what's—" I jerked to a halt when I saw what was lying on my bed. Then I let loose with a few choice four-letter words.

"That's not a flashlight part," Connor said over my shoulder.

"No," I agreed.

"That's not yours, even."

"No."

"Where did you find it?"

I gulped. "In the burial chamber rubble." Kneeling down next to my cot, I reached out with trembling fingers and took the object in my hand. What I'd thought was a handle seemed to be made of some kind of black stone. At first glance I thought it was broken, but in the low light of the tent its smooth surface gleamed and I realized it had deliberately been fashioned with a small gap.

"It's a bracelet," whispered Connor. He reached out and took the object from me. He turned it over several times before taking my hand in his and slipping the hard black ring around my wrist. "Onyx. See?"

"But . . ." I rotated the stone so that the blue knob at the top sat atop my wrist. It wasn't the prettiest bracelet I'd seen. Hieroglyphs ran down its edges. I traced over them with my finger, recognizing the combination of the glyphs for reeds, a half circle, two slash marks, and a familiar animal. "That's for the Egyptian god Set. And what's this bird decoration?"

"Lapis." Connor looked at me, eyes wide. "Set. Chloe, I don't think you're supposed to have this," he said. "Don't you recognize it?"

My insides felt cold and clammy. "No. Should I?"

"Yes!" he exclaimed. "Weren't you at lunch Wednesday when Dr. Tousson announced that there'd been a theft from the artifacts trailer? I think it was this bracelet!"

"I missed lunch twice this week because Dr. Battista kept me," I said. I didn't like the look in his eyes. I hadn't stolen anything! "Is this really . . . you don't think that I . . ."

"No!" he said. "You wouldn't! But where did you get it?"

"Down in the burial chamber, the night that Seth and I . . . well, you know." It was ridiculous to think I'd found a stolen bracelet. Wasn't it? Connor had to be mistaken. "It was buried in the rubble and I thought it was part of your flashlight when I pocketed it. Are you sure this is it?"

"I don't know," he said. "I wasn't paying much attention. It's not like any of us go to the artifacts trailer. That's conservation team territory. But if it is . . . I could ask the other kids."

"And draw attention?" Was he crazy? "Why not just shine a big spotlight on me and write the word *thief* on my forehead! Here, here's some lip gloss! Do it!"

"Don't make jokes," he said. "This is pretty serious, you know."

"Trust me!" I was near hysteria. "I know!"

When the tent flap opened for a second time that evening, I was grateful to have Connor near. He turned and stood in front of me. I used him as a shield while I slipped the bracelet off my hand and into my pocket, and tried to compose my face. "What are you two doing?" Kathy Klemper asked with definite suspicion. She walked to her cot and removed a smart little pith helmet from her head and put it on her pillow. She had looked as if she were about to lead an honors club safari. "You're up to mischief."

"We were just getting sweaters," Connor told her without a hint of warmth.

"You're hiding something." She craned her neck to glare at me.

"No, we're not," we both said in unison again. We looked at each other, both plainly uncomfortable.

Kathy sniffed. "You're bad liars."

Two things were clear: One, we were going to have to get rid of this bracelet. And two, we were definitely going to have to practice our conspiratorial skills, if we both expected to last through the month's end.

Six

The blood had more or less coagulated around the jagged slash on my forearm by the time Dag arrived from camp bearing a first-aid kit. At least it had stopped running down my arm and dripping off my fingers. While I'd waited, I had pet one of the pack of unowned mongrel puppies playing near the slab of rock where I sat. It was a friendly little dog, even though its eyes were crusty with sand and surrounded by flies. When it started to lick the soft part of my arm where I'd sliced myself on a metal wire, I wasn't sure whether or not to make it stop. The long white streak where the dog's tongue had slurped across my arm was the cleanest I'd seen it in days.

Dag, however, scrubbed so hard at my fresh wound with the alcohol patch that it started to ooze again. I winced at the sting of it. "Do not be making faces with squinted eyes," she ordered, scouring off three or four vital layers of epidermis. "You are lucky that you are not dead! Working so close to dead mummies! Disturbing rest of a thousand years!"

"Several thousand," I said automatically, then wished I'd kept my mouth shut. Dagmar hated to be corrected. She used her teeth to rip a long strip from the adhesive tape roll, then wrapped it around my arm, tourniquet-like, cutting off the blood supply to my fingers. I supposed the tape held the gauze over the cut, but it was so tight that if I didn't adjust it in a few minutes, I was going to need an amputation.

"Is not mattering how old a curse is, is still a curse!" she said. From inside her Dig Egypt! T-shirt she withdrew a small gold crucifix on a chain, kissed it, and dropped it back in. Because, you know, every woman should put her lips on a dirty chunk of metal that's been hanging between her sweaty mammaries all day. Right. "Look at you!"

When she waved her hand in my direction, I realized she was right. The fresh cut on the underside of my left forearm matched the slice I'd given my right shin with my trowel; both cuts nicely complemented the scrape on my cheek from where I'd tripped against a wall two days before. The mighty purple-and-brown bruise on my calf I'd gotten . . . well, I scarcely remembered. Over the past week I'd been so accident-prone I was a one-girl episode of *E.R.* "It's just clumsiness, not curses," I muttered, pulling at the bandage a little to see if there was still feeling in my limb. "Dumb luck."

"Is mummy's curse upon you!" Dag sat back on the slab and nodded over what she thought was a bandaging job well done. Personally I thought it looked like a Brownie troop project gone horribly wrong, but at least now that she had finished I didn't have to smell the hair spray that kept Dag's big red wedge in place. "None of other Dig Egypt! childrens have such luck! This is the proof that curse of the mummies is working against Chloe Bryce!"

"Dag, there is no such thing—"

The chaperone pulled from a backpack adorned with the

Swedish flag an apple, which she rubbed on her Dig Egypt! tee. Dagmar had designed the Dig Egypt! logo herself: Nefertari wearing sunglasses and giving the thumbs-up sign. Need I add that none of us ever wore the awful things? She crunched into the fruit with her enormous front teeth. I wonder from which half of the family she got those things: Tyrannosaurus or rabid killer bunny? "When the tomb of Tutankhamen was being found by Carter and Carnarvon, description of curses were being read everywhere in the tomb! And like that!" She snapped her finger, bit into the apple, and spoke while chewing. "Everyone dead!"

"Carnarvon died, yes, but his daughter went into the tomb with him when it was opened and she lived until 1980," I pointed out. "Most of the people present at that tomb opening lived to old age."

Dag didn't want to listen to logic, though. I let her ramble on about curses and mummies and trick locks treated with ancient anthrax spores, hoping that if I kept my reactions to a minimum, she'd eventually get tired and wander away. I didn't believe a single word, of course.

Not out in the broad daylight, anyway. Once I went back down that ladder and into the tomb, though, the hairs prickling on the back of my neck might tell me another story. And, of course, there was the constant reminder of the bracelet hanging around my neck on a knotted length of twine. Maybe it was cursed, I reflected. After all, the night before, Connor and I had thought that the easiest way to get rid of a possibly stolen artifact I wasn't even supposed to have touched, much less taken and kept stuffed under my cot all week, would be simply to sneak it back into the pile of loose flood rubble where I'd found it. Easy, right?

Wrong. This morning I'd arrived in the burial chamber to

find a man sitting in my spot. Naeem, one of the locals, was using his trowel and brush to work his way through the debris, dumping the refuse into one of the recycled-tire baskets sitting at his side. In my spot! *My* spot! The spot where I'd planned to rebury the stupid bracelet! I'd even practiced with Connor my expressions of surprise at unearthing it. *Dr. Battista! Come look!*

Dr. Battista, though, had other plans for me this morning. Note taking, to be specific. "I want you to be my factotum," she announced. You didn't disobey Dr. Battista. Oh, no. Not when she was so stern, and so totally cool, and not even when your stolen bracelet was knocking a dent in your sternum and you didn't have a dictionary around to look up the word *factotum.* She handed me a laptop computer, sat me on a little field stool behind her, and had me type in her notes and measurements as she took them. In the afternoon, Dr. Jumoke and another expert had me take down their translations of the hieroglyphics they were uncovering. I felt a little like the stenographer to the gods, but at least it wasn't as dirty as the digging.

Only problem was, Naeem stayed hunkered down over the rubble—my rubble!—leaving only when he attached his basket to the rope a few feet away. Since he was Muslim, he wasn't even going to break for a meal until sunset. The only shot I really had at fobbing off that onyx bracelet would be to toss it over Dr. Battista's head like a basketball and hope it landed in the sarcophagus without breaking. And, of course, hope they didn't notice. Fat chance. Even I couldn't look that innocent.

While Dag had been eating and talking . . . and spitting, unfortunately . . . some of the Egyptian laborers clearing debris from around the tomb left their lines to stand around us, muttering to each other. One of them made an angry gesture in Dag's direction, furrowing his eyebrows and making a motion toward his mouth.

Dag stopped chewing. Her eyes grew wide. She cringed and folded in on herself; the corners of her lips began to tremble. To look at her you might have thought she was about to lose her maidenly flower to some rough Arab sheik. Like anyone would be that desperate! The men weren't threatening in that way at all. They were dissatisfied about something, that's for sure, but they weren't about to attack.

"Oh," I said, finally guessing what they meant from their gestures at the apple. Dr. Battista had told us our first night. "It's Ramadan," I reminded her. Dag looked at me blankly. "Ramadan, the Muslim holiday. Muslims fast all day and don't eat until nighttime."

"I am not following the Muslim way."

"But it's rude to eat in front of them during Ramadan, when they can't eat," I told her. I grappled for some way to make her understand. "It's disrespectful. It's like inviting a Jewish family over for a ham dinner." The blank look on her face only made me more frustrated. Between all the nonsense about curses and her utter stupidity, not to mention the water-rationing issue, it felt more as if I were chaperoning Dag than the other way around. "Just put it . . . Stop being so stupid! Oh, *give* me the apple."

It took a moment to pry it from her fingers. She was so intent on jerking her head around to keep an eye on all the upset Muslims that she scarcely seemed to notice. When I finally had the remainder of the fruit tucked away in the outer pocket of her backpack, the men's grumbling noticeably diminished. After half a minute they all wandered off back to their chores—save for one really old man with a long beard and sunken cheeks. He kept muttering to himself and brushing his chin with the back of his hand. Even he eventually went back to the chain of men passing baskets of debris from one to another. "See?" I told the chaperone.

Dagmar looked absolutely stunned. "I am not believing it," she finally said, shaking her head. She hoisted up her pack to her lap. For a moment I was afraid she might haul out the apple again and start the whole thing over, but instead she pulled out a pad and a pen and began scribbling.

"It's a cultural thing," I explained. "But I'm sure you know— What's that?" She had ripped the topmost slip from her pad and brandished it at me. I'd gotten my driver's license only four months before and (despite my mom's darkest predictions) hadn't yet gotten a ticket, but Rona McDonald's dramatic flourish brought to mind a police officer nailing a speeder with a hefty fine. *Official Warning,* the slip said at the top. Underneath it was marked with the date and the words, *Chloe Bryce: Insub, impud, insol.* "You've got to be kidding."

"Three warnings will be sending you home from the Dig Egypt! project without the letter official of credit," she informed me stiffly.

Once I took a kickball to the solar plexus and for a half hour felt like I couldn't breathe. This moment felt a lot like that one. "Why?!"

"The insubordination, the impudence, the insolence. You should be holding the tongue in the right mouth!" I gaped at her accusation. "Warning number two this would be if not for intervention of Tousson boy." Who? Oh. Seth. That. I'd nearly gotten a warning that night? When I opened my mouth to protest, she held up a finger. "Dagmar Sorensson is not stupid! She is speaking the fourteen languages, good in all, and has studied at Oxford University! In England!"

"I know where Oxford is!" I sputtered. The second the

words left my lips, I felt my skin flush. Was that what she meant by my tongue in the wrong mouth? Just contradicting her? Or was it some weird reference to kissing? But she had clearly been in the wrong with the apple! I had *saved* her from some major cultural blowup. She didn't see that?

"Now is moment for spending time on mending the bridge." She slid from the slab while I tried to figure out that one. "Why are you not being good girl, like Kathy Klemper, eh? Perhaps is being best to send you home before you are having more of the accidents!"

My legs couldn't help but tremble as I watched her stalk back in the direction of camp. Dagmar just didn't understand. I didn't get into trouble. I *never* got into trouble. Scrapes and escapades were for other people, not for Chloe Bryce! For sixteen years I had been the good girl. The quiet girl. I was the little sister who stood aside and watched her brothers get the spankings and the notes from the principal. I was the student in class who didn't sit too near the back with the troublemakers or too close to the front with the teacher's pets, the girl who got very good grades and never dared mess around in the classroom. I was the one who sat still and never fell asleep in church, the one who always remembered her thank-you notes after Christmas, the one who washed her hands and kept her room clean and followed instructions and combed her hair and didn't bite her nails, and now I was getting a warning for *insub, impud, insol* and it hadn't even been my fault!

Insubordination! I'd never been accused of a six-syllable crime before!

I wanted to kick something. Actually, I first wanted to throw something at Dagmar's receding Brillo-pad head and then follow up with a kick to her kneecaps. At least then if

I was being accused of insubordination I'd have something to show for it.

I didn't do any of those things, though. I was Chloe Bryce, professional good girl. After sixteen years of praise and smiles I had just gotten my first red mark. It hurt, and I didn't know what to do about it. I stuffed the citation in my pocket and slowly shuffled into the tomb, back to work in its darkest depths.

That seemed appropriate. .

I'm not sure how Dr. Battista noticed I wasn't at my best. Maybe it was the look in my eyes, haunted and lonely. Maybe it was my long-suffering sighs. Or maybe, just maybe, it was the fact that she rattled off an entire document's worth of facts and figures about the fiber count in the first mummy's shroud before she noticed I hadn't heard a word of it. I was sitting there staring off into space and feeling miserable when finally she raised my chin up with the tip of her wooden pointer. "Chloe?" Her dark and narrow eyebrows arched high.

For the second time that afternoon I felt my skin redden. At least down there in the dark it wasn't readily visible. "Oh, man, I am so sorry," I apologized. Maybe I could pick up the thread again. "Um. Something about linen."

"Something is occupying you. What is it?" She crossed her bone-thin arms and waited. Most magazines about fashion and glamour always focus on girls who are only a little older than I. They're usually a lot skinnier, too, and wear serial-killer expressions. And people call that beautiful? They hadn't seen Dr. Battista.

I guessed Dr. Battista was in her late forties at the very least. She had gray streaking her wild, wavy hair. Her eyes were too small and black—you might even say beady—and her eyebrows too thin. Her skin was both naturally dark and even further tanned by years of sun. She'd never appear in any fashion magazine, but she really was so, so beautiful. Even though Anca Battista was a small woman, she had a way of speaking and moving that made people want to obey her. I couldn't resist that air of command. "Nothing. Only. Well . . ."

I have a complaint about grown-ups, here. Those guys really know how to screw kids up with their conflicting advice, and screw them up good. It starts off young with *Don't dawdle!* combined with *Cool your jets! Why're you in such a hurry?* Then it's *Violence is not the answer*, faced off with *Why don't you stick up for yourself?* From there it's off to *Nobody likes a tattle tale*, versus *Why didn't you tell us something was wrong?* By the time you're my age, don't try to take a lifetime's worth of contradictory advice to heart, or else you'll end up stark, raving bonkers, like me.

I didn't know how to answer Dr. Battista. Did I tell her about Dag and ask her to intervene? Was that tattling? Maybe she'd be one of those adults-should-stick-together types and side with Dag if I mentioned it. Maybe word would even get back to Mophead that I'd tried to get her into trouble, and I'd get another warning. There was even the ominous possibility that if I whined to Anca Battista about my citation, she'd think less of me. I couldn't stand that. And then there was this bracelet. . . .

"I don't think I'm cut out to be an archaeologist," I moaned.

Her expression didn't change. "Close your eyes," she commanded. I blinked and stared. She tapped me gently on my cheek with her long pointer. "Close your eyes. Now," she instructed as I did, "tell me what I'm wearing."

"What?" I thought about it a minute. It was some kind

of game. "You've got on khaki slacks, a dark cotton blouse with the sleeves rolled up, brown boots." She didn't say anything, so I kept going. "There's a silver clasp in your hair, just between your shoulder blades." Still nothing. "And I think I saw a jacket lying on the ground."

"Where am I standing?" she asked. "Keep your eyes closed."

"Next to the sarcophagus?" Exactly what did she expect of me? I didn't understand. "Do you want me to describe that, too?"

I heard her take a few steps, and then she spoke again. "Where am I now?"

What was I supposed to be, psychic? "I don't know!"

"Where am I? Describe it," she demanded from somewhere over to my right. Her voice was calm and steady.

I thought about it, playing back in my mind the sound of her footsteps. Four of them, crunching across the grit on the stone floor. "I think you're at the part of the tomb where there's an alcove. It's hard to see in the dark, but it looks like a painting of the god with a beetle for his head? Kheperi?" He was the god of the sunrise, or something like that. "There are painted columns on either side?" Again I heard the crunch of her boots across the floor, and again she asked me to name her location. I guessed her to be standing between the two sarcophagi, then again over by the plastered-over passageway to a room they hadn't opened yet, and finally, judging by the weird way her voice sounded and the way Naeem stopped working, beneath the burial shaft.

Finally I felt the tip of her pointer on my forehead again. I opened my eyes and found her looking down at me, hands on my hips. "So that you know, you were correct each time. Awareness, Chloe, is what a person needs to become an archaeologist. Awareness, an avid curiosity, the ability to piece together information into a credible narrative with very few clues, and the skill to communicate it to those who cannot be there. We are storytellers, creating histories from scraps of clay and languages thousands of years dead. I believe you have those qualities," she said in a way that made clear that no matter what anyone else thought, she was the authority on this matter.

"You do? You think that just because I could figure out where you were?" She nodded. "This is where you teach me how to use the Force for good and not for evil, right?"

She ignored my pathetic joke. "You have a quality of observation that is important. You see things with both the inner and the outer eyes. That is essential. Whether or not you choose to be an archaeologist in the future is up to you. But while you are here, you *are* an archaeologist. I would be glad to have you at any excavation where I'm working." Before I could glow too much from that compliment, however, she added, "Unless I can find a replacement who would actually type out the notes I give to her."

"Okay, okay!" I settled the laptop back onto my knees, grinning a little. For the first time since the incident outside, I relaxed a bit. It was nice to know that I was wanted somewhere.

Still. Three words haunted me all afternoon. *Insub, impud, insol!*

That night Sue repeated them aloud. "They sound like a spell from Harry Potter. *Ils ressemblent à d'un enchantment du Hogwarts.*"

Whenever Sue nearly got a sentence right, Mallorie always grew visibly excited. *"Ah! J'adore la série des* Harry Potter! *Je me précipite pour les acheter au moment où ils sortent en librairie!* Ron Weasley *est bien mignon celui du film . . . avez-vous vu le film?* Draco Malfoy *me donne lachair de poule. J'ai trop hâte au prochain livre!"*

A terrible pause filled my old tent.

"Did anyone understand what she just said?" Bo asked through his teeth, which were formed into a polite smile.

We all wore those polite smiles. "It sounded like something about Harry Potter?" I replied, trying not to move my lips.

Deidre hissed, "Someone say something!"

"Oui?" Sue ventured. When Mallorie nodded vigorously, we all relaxed and nodded. *"Oui! Oui!"* we repeated over and over again like lunatics. *"Oui!"*

"That poor girl is going to go home knowing even less than when she arrived." Sue opened her mouth at my remark, so I added quickly, "Don't translate that." She shut it again. "So what should I do?"

Connor, his bare feet squirming in the sand as he sat on my abandoned cot, looked over the citation once again. He flipped it over and back, then shook his head. "I think you should just talk to Dag. She's got to be a pretty reasonable person or they wouldn't have hired her, right? You know, be a little timid, be a little meek. You can manage it."

I started to nod, but even as the muscles went into motion, my neck stiffened. Of all the things to say to me, why tell me I could manage timidity? "What do you mean by that?"

"You know."

"Oh, do I?" Suddenly I felt as if I had a tiny ball of molten lava buried between my shoulder blades. Maybe it was the awful cots, or the afternoons spent perched on a little field stool with no back. Then again, maybe it was the suspicion that Connor had known all along I was never a part of

North Seattle High's popular set. Whatever the cause, stress was catching up with me in a big way. "What exactly are you saying?" I challenged.

"Overreact much?" he asked me. "I'm just saying you can pretend, that's all. You know. Tone it down." He narrowed his shoulders and looked up at an imaginary Dag with puppy-dog eyes. "Don't be so *Chloe*." He flexed his biceps and pretended to be stomping around.

Somehow that only made me angrier. "So now my name's an adjective for the Incredible Hulk?"

"*Le* Hulk Incredible," I heard Sue whisper, heavy on the *bluh*.

"No, but you've got to admit, you've got a reputation," Connor said.

I wasn't sure what to make of any of this talk. It seemed like he was trying to make peace with me, implying I'd misunderstood him at first, but either way I ended up insulted. "Is that what you guys think of me?" I asked the room. "That I'm some kind of big enormous personality who . . . I don't know! What are you telling me? I'm some kind of loudmouthed, brash, pushy monster?"

No one said anything for a minute. Maybe I'd spoken in French and they didn't know what to make of it? I half expected Bo to rasp out through a smile, just as he had with Mallorie, *Did anyone understand what she just said?* Nope, French was one of the few things that was never going to appear on my college résumé. They'd understood me, all right. They just couldn't deny my words.

Sue tried. "You're not a monster," she said, wrinkling her nose. "You just get things done."

"You're not a monster!" Connor echoed. "You're more of a hurricane force."

I blinked.

"Like when you jumped that burial shaft," Bo added.

"You're like a superhero," Deidre said. "Like when you took care of that scorpion."

"*De que parlons-nous?*" Mallorie asked.

When I stood up, I felt unsteady. "I need some air," I complained.

"But we were going to play cards!" Sue protested. I could tell she was worried about me; she probably thought she'd said something out of line.

"Everything's okay," I said, trying to smile. I faked a yawn, too. "You know I haven't gotten any sleep in a few days. Maybe I can slip in a few hours before Dag and Kathy start the snore-fest. Everything's cool," I assured her. "Night, guys."

I relished being alone in the chilly night air outside. Night in Egypt was the one time of the day when I didn't feel sweaty and miserable. I could lift my arms to the stars and let them feel the coolness, without anyone making any comments about how stinky I was. Without the sun to heat me or the sight of sand to remind me of my dirty skin, I almost felt normal again. From my pocket I pulled out my wand of gloss and absentmindedly guided it around the contour of my lips.

At the edge of the cliff I paused. The way the waning moon hung over the landscape, its light casting the rippling hills below into a dark relief, made the view look like a postcard. *Egypt by night,* I thought. *Having a miserable time. Wish you were here.*

"Hey." I swiveled around. Somehow Connor, with his soft footfall, had sneaked up behind me. I turned back to look at the landscape. Part of me was glad he'd come; another part was still puzzled and hurt at the curious things he had said in the tent moments before. "Are you mad?" he asked.

"No. Yes. I don't know." I felt confused and miserable. This was seriously the worst night of my life. I would rather experience twelve more transatlantic flights, an afternoon of the tallest roller coasters in the world, a hundred hypodermic needles, and speaking in front of a school assembly. Impromptu. In the nude. Just like in all my nightmares. Only in my nightmares there was always a scary clown in the front row, laughing at me. "It's just weird, finding out how people think about you." I crossed my arms. I didn't want to look at him.

"Chloe, I never called you the Incredible Hulk." When I didn't respond, he sighed. "Why are you worried about what people think about you, anyway? You do fine."

"Why am I worried?" I nearly shouted. My jagged voice sliced through the night, then quickly vanished without echo. "That's all I think about. My entire life has been about what other people think of me. Everything I've done since I've arrived in Egypt has been . . ." There were a lot of ways I could finish that sentence. *Stupid. Senseless. Dumb.* "I'm so mixed up. You guys see me as something I never thought I was. Dagmar sees me as the world champion of the tongue of insolence. Dr. Battista sees me as . . . This whole thing is stupid. I should never have come to Egypt."

"Don't say that," Connor stepped closer. "You don't mean it."

"Oh, yes, I do." Coffee's bitterness could never compete with mine at that moment.

"No, you don't. You shouldn't. You're in your element here. This whole project was made for people like you and me. We're the ones who *want* to be here." There he was again, seeing me as something I wasn't. I didn't want to be here in the Valley of the Servitors. I never had. I was the world's biggest fake—a loser whose entire knowledge of ancient Egypt had been cobbled together from Discovery Channel specials and could fit on the head of a pin. The minute he found out I wasn't like him, he'd run far away and never talk to me again. "You know you're worthy. I know it. So why fret about what other people think?"

"I don't know," I said, miserable and sorry for myself. "I can't help it."

"There are too many people to worry about!" He laughed at me. I knew he was trying to make me feel better. "Why not worry about what only one person thinks of you?"

"Who?" I tried to think of who he might mean. Dr. Battista?

"Me."

"You?" I turned to him then, sniffling before my nose started to run.

Once again he stepped closer. His hands rose to his head and, to my utter astonishment, they skimmed off his baseball cap. He curled the brim and stuck it into his back pocket, ran a few fingers through his dark curls, and then wiped his hands on his shirt. Connor took off his cap? For me? "Don't you care what I think about you?" he asked softly.

"What do you think about me?"

"I think this." He stepped forward, put his hands on my upper arms, and pressed his lips to mine.

At first all I could think to do was compare this kiss to my last. Seth's lips had been fuller and softer than Connor's; they had seemed to probe and push at my own with an expertise that Connor didn't seem to have. Connor was clumsier and more tentative. At one point he even pulled away slightly and laughed, as if surprised that I kissed him back. Then he leaned into me again and I felt his hand under my shirt, warm and solid on the small of my back.

This was much, much better. At that moment I banished Seth from my head forevermore.

"I think about doing this all the time," said Connor into my ear, after he took away his lips. I tingled with chills at the sensations as he nipped my earlobe. "I think about a lot of other things too. You're a part of all of them."

"Oh." Under the influence of a massive tingle attack, it was all I could really say. It came out not really so much a word as a groan.

"You're sweet," he said, nuzzling his way down my neck.

"You're sweet too."

"No, your lips," he whispered. "You taste like fruit."

"Marionberry?" I asked him.

"That could be it."

"Connor?"

"What?"

"Too much talking," I told him. "Not enough kissing."

We didn't say much after that. It was seriously the best night of my life.

I was so giddy and light-headed when my legs finally braided their way back to the big tent that even the sight of Kathy Klemper in a white nightgown with a little pink ribbon at the neck didn't bug me. Have you ever seen that scene in *My Fair Lady* when Audrey Hepburn flits around the room saying she could have danced all night and even begged for more? That was me, only without the flitting, the begging, the dubbed singing, the orchestra, or the really good Belgian cheekbones.

Kathy watched me with a curled lip as I changed into my sweatpants. "I know what you've been doing," she said at last.

"Oh, really?" If I had held out my arms right then, good

and glowing and lovely as I felt, little Disney animated blue-birds might have helped me into a fresh T-shirt. "That's nice."

The curled lip turned into a definite sneer. "You're such a slut."

A while ago that comment might have been the whipped cream and maraschino doggie turd on top of a truly crap-tacular day. Now, though? Rolled off me like water from a duck. "Oh, Kathy," I said with a degree of feigned sadness. "Don't be bitter. Maybe someday you'll find a man who can appreciate you. There must be some blind deaf-mutes out there who won't cringe at the prospect of holding your bony little hand."

"Oh, ha, ha, ha. You make me sick. I'm going to tell Ms. Sorensson on you."

Her mood-killing threat got my attention. I stood up and faced her, hands on my hips. "Exactly how old are you, Kathy?" I asked. "Because you're acting like you're the fourth-grade room monitor, and both of us finished fourth grade a long time ago."

"I'm old enough to know that you think you're hot poop when you're really just a cold fart." Still firmly in the fourth grade, I saw. It must have been a traumatic year for her or something. "Ms. Sorensson and I both see through you!"

"Oh, do you?" My voice was a little louder now. "Well, that's just great. That's all I need watching my every move—you and one scary old woman who'd better keep an eye on the sky for falling houses."

When Kathy smirked in the direction behind me, I experienced a sinking feeling deep in my bowels. Kathy had indeed been seeing right through me. Right through me to the tent flap, where Dagmar stood with a look that could have soured tapioca pudding.

Imp, ins, disresp, read my second and next-to-last citation when Dag tossed it onto my curled-up form on the cot. I pulled the blanket over my shoulders and let the slip of paper drift to the ground, screwing shut my eyes and hoping that the sounds of snoring might drown out the seething in my brain.

Seven

I had heard a lot of pretty cool noises since arriving in Egypt. There'd been the sounds of singing during that confusing night in Cairo after we'd arrived, and its crowds during the days. At night, from the far side of the site where the Muslim workers camped, we'd sometimes hear strains of music from their radios or the scratchy strings of a violin accompanying songs traditionally sung during Ramadan. I'd heard silence, or near-silence, for what I think was the first time in my life, during quiet moments when I walked outside the camp by myself late at night.

Nothing in the entire world could have been sweeter to my ears, though, than the sound of liquid from the water tank trickling into a shallow plastic tray in the bath shed. It made me want to jump up and down and cry all at the same time, just like I would have at age ten on Christmas morning if I'd run downstairs to find under the tree the one present I most wanted—a darned pony.

It was Sunday, our day off. And it was bath time. My first in thirteen days! Mallorie and I were both more or less totally unclothed in the tiny little wooden shack, waiting for the trays to fill with the outside-temperature water, while

Sue sat on a little pile of her own dirty clothes, keeping an eye out to make sure no one opened the shed door. "Are you sure you want to wash those in our dirty water?" I asked her for about the twelfth time that morning.

"You just get the first batch of water nice and sudsy," she assured me. "I'll wash my stuff in that, and then rinse them in your rinse water."

"But we're *filthy*." I rubbed my thumb across my forearm to illustrate. It left behind a grayish streak. "You'll just be getting this stuff all over your clothes."

"Chloe," she said, looking at me levelly, "your dirt couldn't be any worse than what's on there."

I recognized the desperation in her voice. I felt the same way. I hated to admit it, but I was a spoiled little American girl. I liked my water hot, my baths daily, and my hair squeaky-clean. In Egypt, the only things hot were my armpits, and the only things I got daily were bug bites and a backache. The only things nice and clean were Kathy Klemper and Dagmar Sorensson . . . only not so much on the *nice* part.

One sponge bath every two weeks would have seemed like a punishment at home, but here it was an absolute, giggle-worthy luxury.

Once we'd filled our first pans of water, Mallorie and I went to work on shampooing each other's hair. It was wonderful. It was the absolute best my head had ever felt. I didn't care that we didn't have shampoo and that we had to use a nasty old bar of soap so brown and full of grit and ash that it looked like it had been dug up from one of the pyramids. My requirements were few. It was soap. It felt soapy. It made suds. And it was wonderful.

Both Mallorie and I had similar short haircuts, so once we'd soaped up our heads and let our scalps begin basking in the lather, we used folded-up scraps of cloth to start soaping up. Mallorie was so happy that she was near tears. I sighed. "We are probably the only girls I have ever known who fantasize about bathing."

Sue sighed. "And clean clothes."

"*Ceci se sent si bon!*" said Mallorie.

"I heard the conservation team gets daily baths."

"I wouldn't doubt it," I told Sue. Jan James had seemed mighty clean compared to me, the day she'd invaded my tent. "No wonder they call us grunts and slobs and all kinds of names. Okay, Sue, go for it."

"Yay!" Sue hopped up and plunged her duds into what was left of my soapy water, which was already so murky that it looked like I'd collected and melted the slushiest, dirtiest roadside snow I could find. "Thank God that in the desert these will dry in *no* time. Um, *thanquerrie le Dieu quelle le* stuff *sera dryez-vous rapidement.*"

I knelt down to help Sue with the last of her T-shirts. Soap bubbles crackled and popped in my ears. "Ready to rinse? *La nouvelle eau*?" I asked when we were all finished, and had poured the filthy water down into the trench at the shed's far end. They both nodded.

Mallorie and I were allowed one more pan of water each for rinsing. I twisted the faucet carefully, as I reckoned the plumbing leading to the water tower directly above us had been installed back when Napoleon invaded Egypt. The trickle of water we expected never came. I twisted harder. Then, from overhead, we all heard the familiar sound of groaning pipes and the screech of the empty tank.

The heck! "Nooooooo!" I yelled, wanting to beat my head against the shed wall.

"What? No! No! No!" Sue looked as if she were about to murder someone.

"*Que se produit?*" Mallorie wanted to know.

It was no use. I kept twisting and turning my valve without any result save for an impromptu organ concert from the water tank. Only when I finally turned the valve shut and bit my lip to keep from crying did I remember I was still soapy all over. "My skin!" As the soap on it started to dry, my skin started to itch. And pull.

"*Mes cheveux!*" Mallorie suddenly put her hands to her head, still scrunchy from the shampoo. I realized that the soap was drying in my hair as well, making it stiffer by the moment.

"My undies!" Sunita wailed, and began to paw through her pile of laundry. "They're all wet! And soapy! And *gross!* What are we going to do?"

Both of the girls looked at me expectantly. Who was I? Moses, who could strike a rock with his staff and make water gush out? I didn't think so. I was as bewildered and upset as they were. What did they expect from me? I shrugged.

We all stared at each other in absolute horror for a few moments. Then, without warning, Mallorie grabbed a handful of wet laundry, including Sue's favorite tee with the word *princess* silk-screened onto it, from the table and threw it to the floor. Dirty suds arced up and above us, splatting against the shed wall. "*Ah, putain! C'est la dernière goutte! J'en ai marre de l'Égypte! J'en ai marre du sable! Marre de ne pas avoir assez d'eau pour prendre un bain!*" she yelled, not seeming to care that we couldn't understand her. "*Marre de cette nourriture infecte! Marre de vivre avec ces gens bizarres qui me traietent comme une imbécile et ne comprennent pas un mot de ce que je leur dis! J'aimerais mieux qu'on me mène au plein milieu du désert et qu'on me laisse aux rapaces?!*"

Sue and I took a quick look at each other, then stared back at Mallorie. I didn't need to know what she'd said. I knew just how she felt. Laundry abuse is, after all, pretty much the universal language. "You poor baby," I said to her, trying to brush her short dark hair from her eyes.

"*Pauvre fille!*" Sue echoed, suddenly not at all seeming to mind about her princess shirt soaking the floor. Mallorie looked so hopeless and close to crying, and Sue so upset, that I knew I had to do something. They'd expected a reaction from me for a pretty simple reason: In their minds I was the kind of girl who'd actually *do* something about this situation.

I'd come to Egypt planning to be someone I wasn't. Someone who was brave and never flinched or cringed from the scary stuff. I'd thought it would be fun to be someone else for a change—to shed a skin I'd grown tired of. I hadn't realized I'd have to take on new responsibilities, too.

I could have shirked those duties right then. I surely wanted to. Yet I knew deep down that something had to be done, and that I should be the one to take charge.

That's how I ended up leading a march across camp—a little parade of what resembled archaeological circus clowns. Mallorie and I were dressed in nothing more than our lightweight little bathrobes and flip-flops, our hair so stiff from the drying soap that it was standing straight up and forward on our heads. We looked a little bit like refugees from some awful 1980s synthesizer hair band. Behind us stumbled Sue, her arms full of wet and increasingly heavy laundry. Behind her were Bo and Connor and Deidre, who had heard Mallorie's shrieking and had been hovering outside the bath shed hoping that no one had been murdered. Those of us at the head of the parade got the most attention. When we stalked through the little cluster of larger tents where the junior archaeologists sat in lounge chairs reading or listening to music or playing dominoes, the men and women there reeled back in such astonishment that they couldn't laugh until after we'd tramped by. We rounded the artifacts storage and headed straight for the trailer directly behind.

I knocked on the door. No, let's be honest: I *pounded*.

Through the flipped-up windows along the trailer's length, I could hear voices in conversation, followed by footsteps. "Hey, we're in the middle of—" Eddie Loret stuck his head out the door. At the sight of me, fright hair and everything, he blinked rapidly. Then he took in the sight of the rest of our team, arms crossed, faces hostile. "Gang, I can see something's up, but . . ."

"You bet something's up," Connor said from the back. I appreciated his support. None of this was easy for me.

". . . but Dr. B. and I are in the middle of a meeting with some officials from Cairo—"

"Eddie," I interrupted him, "we aren't going away. This is serious. There is a thief in our midst."

The excavation team's second-in-command seemed shaken by my announcement. The trailer shook; Eddie had to move out of the way as several people pushed their way out behind him. Three Egyptian guys in dark and spotless suits burst from inside like they'd been shot by cannons, followed by both Dr. Jumoke and a tired-looking Dr. Battista. When I looked at the other kids, a couple of them wore frightened expressions on their faces. Mallorie didn't have a clue what was going on, and there was really no way to explain it to her. Connor, though, seemed resolute, and so did Sue.

Eddie cleared his throat and looked at the other adults. "Chloe, this is Mr. Massad, and Mr. Amhari, and Dr.

Kharima, from the Supreme Council of Antiquities. Now, theft's a pretty serious accusation. I hope you're not joking."

"I wouldn't joke, not about this," I said. I was getting a little nervous, myself. Why would these Council of Antiquities guys have any interest in water rationing? "It's been happening for a while now, and we're all tired of it. Right, guys?"

I was thankful my little posse didn't fail me. When they agreed with head shakes and "yeahs!" and one "damn right" from Bo, I suddenly felt like I could go through with this. Dr. Battista, too, nodded encouragingly at me. She didn't seem to find it at all odd that I was standing in front of her looking like a lost mutant from the planet Sex Pistol. "Do you know who's been stealing, Chloe?" Eddie asked me in a calm voice. It was almost too calm.

"I do," I said. "It's Dagmar."

"And Kathy Klemper," said Sue.

"But mostly Dagmar." I was sure on that point.

"*Dagmar?*" asked Mr. Massad, pronouncing the word as if he'd chugged down a Pepsi bottle only to find it was full of NyQuil.

"Dagmar Sorensson is the chaperone of the Dig Egypt! project," Dr. Battista explained. "The University of Seattle sponsors a monthlong program that invites some of the brightest young people from across—"

"I know who Dagmar is," Dr. Kharima interrupted. "Why do you accuse her of stealing my country's most precious antiquities?"

Huh? "Dagmar has been stealing antiquities?" I asked, feeling chilled. Oh, God. The bracelet. They'd found out that I'd removed the bracelet. They'd come to arrest me! And I'd walked right into it!

All attention swung around to me again. The three SCOA

guys began talking at once. Dr. Battista held out her long, thin fingers and tried to calm everyone. "You implied she was the one who took the artifact from the locked trailer," she told me.

"No!" I didn't want to talk about that at all! The less said about that issue, the better, until I got rid of the stupid bracelet somehow.

Eddie waited for a quiet moment in the babble. "Hold up, Chloe. A minute ago you told us that Dagmar stole the artifact."

"No, she didn't!" Several of the team stuck up for me.

"I said that Dagmar is stealing *water,*" I told Eddie, still feeling sweaty from my close encounter with arrest. "She is! She and Kathy are always clean when the rest of us are dirty. Even their clothes are way less grungy than the rest of ours."

"Today was supposed to be their bath day, and look at them!" Connor said. "They didn't even get half their quota!"

"Yeah, I mean, they're skankier than when they went in." I could've done without Bo's particular contribution.

"And look at my laundry!" said Sue, shaking her mucky clothes. "It's disgusting!"

There was a confused moment after that when I thought the entire idea of complaining officially to Eddie might have been a bad idea. The Egyptian gentlemen seemed to think that I'd deliberately intended to play some kind of joke on them; Dr. Battista seemed torn between trying to calm them down and herd them indoors and murmuring directions to Eddie. Eddie, in the meantime, couldn't seem to decide whether to be angry or to laugh. By the time Dr. Battista and Dr. Jumoke had ushered the SCOA men back into the trailer, the laughing had taken over.

"I don't think that water theft is funny at all!" I complained.

"No, no, you're right. It's only that you nearly caused a Swedish–Egyptian–U.S. international scandal just now," he said, wiping amused moisture from the corners of his eyes. "It really isn't a humorous matter at all, kids, I'm sorry." There's nothing I hate worse than adults who think that things are funny or dismissible just because a teenager says them. Eddie seemed to be sobering up quickly, though. "Water hoarding is a serious offense in a small community like this one in the desert, especially when we have to import our supplies from so far away. It's hard to balance the water we need for research with water we need for cooking with water for bathing and clean clothes. I'm sorry. It's just that those council guys are here investigating the theft from the artifacts trailer. When they heard you say there was a thief . . ."

Oh. Okay. Now I understood what had been going on. It didn't change anything though. "That's all very well and good," I told him, arms crossed. "But what are you going to do about our situation?"

All six of us were practically daring him to do nothing, just to see what happened. Eddie made some reassuring motions with his hands. "It's okay, guys. A second ago Dr. Battista gave me the go-ahead to special-order another tank—a tank especially for you guys. If I radio in now, the truck can be here in an hour or an hour and a half."

I liked the sound of more water, but I wasn't entirely certain that it would end up on our skins. "How do we know that Dag won't be siphoning off this batch?" I asked.

"I'll tell the drivers to let you have the water right off the truck," he said. "They'll stick around long enough for all of you to get baths and to do all your laundry. Only when you're finished will I have them dump the rest in the tank."

"*Eau!*" Sue translated for Mallorie, who had been waiting patiently during all the talk. The French girl's face lit up. "*Beaucoups de eau!*"

"No way, dude! Baths for everyone?" Bo wanted to know. "Awesome!"

"I could sure use one," Connor agreed.

"My bath day was just three days ago," Deidre said. Sue kicked her.

Despite the muted excitement around me, I had one more question to ask. "And Dagmar?"

Eddie bobbed his head back and forth in the way my parents usually did when they were about to say, *Maybe we will; maybe we won't.* "It's hard to prove hoarding when everyone's on the honor system," he said. Before I could protest, he added, "I'll make some discreet inquiries, though. Okay?"

I supposed it was as good as we were going to get. "We can live with that. Thank you."

"No problem. Let me go radio in the order. You guys can hang out in the mess tent while you're waiting, if you'd rather avoid . . . you know. Rona McDonald."

Oh, man. Had the adults heard my nickname for Dag? How embarrassing. At least Eddie had the decency to wink before he left.

"Water!" said Connor, lifting his arms up to the skies. "Yes!"

"He said we could wash all our clothes, right?"

"Yeah, Bo, and *please* do your socks, man," Connor joked. "Those things be stanking up the tent."

"You're wacked," Bo said. "That stank's probably your *shorts*."

Poor Sue's laundry was about eight times heavier wet than dry, and she'd been carrying it the entire time I'd had my little face-off with the adults. "Let me help," I said, taking some of the clothing. The others divided the load, and soon we were heading back to the center of camp in a giddy mood. I was feeling pretty good, myself. Water! Clean clothes! And hair that didn't feel like someone had peed in it!

"We couldn't have done this without you, Chloe," Sue said to me as we straggled behind the others.

"Not true."

"Whatever. Still. I'm going to fetch the rest of that cesspool known as my wardrobe!" She ran on ahead, tugging Mallorie's hand.

Our little French ambassador gave me pecks on both cheeks. *"Merci, Chloe!"* Mallorie's mood seemed about a thousand times better. She skipped instead of walking, even.

"Bonne nuit!" I called after her.

Connor did a spry little twist on his foot and left Bo's side for mine. "Not meaning to correct you or anything," he said, "but I think you just wished her a good night."

I was in too good a mood to care. "Good night, good morning, good afternoon, what's the diff? Hey."

His stride lurched to a halt. I knew Connor well enough by now to know why he'd stopped. Off to the north, in a view visible only between two solitary tents used to hold supplies, lay the hills. From where we stood, the valley below wasn't visible, but beyond the edge of the plateau was another of Egypt's sunlit picture-perfect views. "Sorry," he said after a minute of gazing out to the horizon.

"No problem," I said, a little shy. Whenever I chanced on Connor in one of his reflective moods, I felt as if I were getting a special glimpse into some very private and personal part of his life. It was even more intimate than the times we'd spent on the edge of the cliff at night, lips pressed against each other. In a way it felt as if I'd stumbled onto his confidential journal; I was too self-conscious to take more than little glimpses at what I saw.

Those moments were dangerous to me, though. They made me want to open myself up to him in return. How would he react, though, if he knew that I was a fake? Even worse, what was going to happen when we both got back home at the end of this trip? You know, pop songs are always going on about how good it feels to have someone to be close to. Why don't they ever talk about the downsides—the doubts, the self-pity, the way you want to ask a guy question after question but make yourself hold back because he'll think you're a total freak if you let them loose?

Don't get me wrong. Kissing Connor and letting him hold me in the cool night air was fantastic. Best feeling ever! How come no one ever, like, gives us even a small warning about all the scary stuff that goes along with the good? Just like I'd found being a better Chloe had its drawbacks, so did being a Chloe who was falling for a guy.

Connor seemed a little shy, too. Could he maybe be thinking some of the same things as me? "So it seems like once again everyone's a little better off because you're around," he said, plunging his hands deep into his pockets.

I turned red. What would he do if I told him what a fake I was? "Nah, not really," I said. "Something would've happened." Should I tell him?

"Hello? I don't think so. Who would have had the nerve to go to Eddie or Dr. Battista? I wouldn't. I don't think any of your girls would've. I know Bo wouldn't. He's scared to death of Dr. B. They all are."

I was surprised at his contradiction. "You would have done something, wouldn't you?"

He shook his head. "No. I wish I could, but I couldn't." When I gaped at him in surprise, he stopped walking and faced me. "I can't afford to draw that kind of attention to myself."

"Why?"

When he paused and shuffled and started several sentences that never made it past his lips, I knew I was in for something big.

"I don't want to get into it with you. It wouldn't be fair."

"Hey," I told him, trying to sound encouraging. "I thought we were friends. And, um. You know. More."

I'd barely finished my sentence when he blurted out, "I shouldn't be here." The words hung between us for a moment. "I shouldn't be here," he repeated. "I'm not . . . It's complicated."

"You feel like . . . like you're here under false pretenses?" He nodded slowly, as if it were difficult for him to admit. Although my words were careful, the Queen of Denial was inside my head, yelling, *I'm the same!* "Maybe you . . ." How could I say it right, so I could lead into my confession? "Maybe you feel like a fake? Is that the way you feel?"

After a long moment so suspenseful I could barely breathe, he nodded. "Yeah. Please don't—"

He didn't have to finish that sentence. "I won't," I told him.

I'm the same! I wanted to say the words so badly that I could practically taste their bitterness. How could he be more of a fake than me?

Something strange happened, though. Connor hadn't even told me what freaky reason he had for feeling fake; it couldn't be because he wasn't smart, or because he didn't know his stuff. Like he told me once, we both knew he was worthy of being here. And yet something was bothering him enough to make him doubt that he belonged. I wanted to tell him that I was the real McCoy, the true freak of nature in this camp. I'd even opened my mouth to say it—but suddenly I realized how relieved he'd seemed when he made his confession. It was as if he'd been dragging one of the stones of the great pyramids all on his own, only to have his burden lightened when I grabbed the rope and pulled with him.

I wanted badly to unload all the doubts I'd had about myself and this trip. I really did. Yet somehow I couldn't bring myself to make his load heavier again by adding my own to it. For the last two weeks I'd tried to pretend I was a better person, a braver Chloe than I used to be. Wouldn't it really make me a better Chloe right this moment if I didn't contribute to whatever was his big burden?

"I'm . . ." I mumbled. In the past I've always thought it was tough to put others ahead of myself. Taking care of the other kids in camp had made me rethink some of my old habits. Somehow, with Connor, it seemed easier still to put aside my own doubts. What I wanted to say could wait until later. "I think we all feel like fakes, to some extent." He nodded, but I could tell he needed reassurance. "I do too. But we're the ones who *should* be here, right? That's what you keep saying, anyway."

Would that do it? Was it a start? When he reached for my hand right then, and squeezed it in thanks, I knew I'd done the right thing.

We resumed our walk and kept quiet until we'd nearly

caught up to the other kids, who were all ransacking their tents for dirty laundry and dragging it into piles near the water shed. I couldn't help but think back to that scary moment a few minutes before, when I'd thought the Supreme Council of Antiquities men might take me away. I was struck by a thought. "You think anyone will ever catch Dag using more than her quota of water?" I asked.

Connor thought seriously for a minute. "I'd like to hope so. But probably not. You think?"

"I don't think they will," I admitted, thinking of the little black bracelet well hidden in my duffel bag. "She's the one who should be caught with that bracelet, not me."

"That would be funny, all right."

"Yeah, it would, wouldn't it?" The idea sounded crazy, but Dag could talk her way out of anything—why not make her weasel out of my predicament? "Connor, you're brilliant!"

A horrified expression gradually took over his face. "I thought you were joking!"

Joking? Me? Maybe I had been. Good-girl Chloe would never have dared such a thing. The more I thought about it, though, the better the idea sounded. So Dag thought I was a bad influence? I'd show her the insubordination, the impudence, and the insolence, all right.

Eight

Meals in the mess tent were the one time of day when everyone on the dig came together like a big family. Only not really. Just like in the six-person Bryce family, there were people who didn't want to be there. Others came only because they had to. And there were many who skipped. The Muslim workers and archaeologists waited for sunset to break their daylong Ramadan fast outside by their campfires. Some of the senior scientists, like Dr. Battista and Dr. Jumoke, either stayed at the dig until after dinner, or stayed so busy in the research trailers that they missed eating altogether. Izumi and Jan usually ate at the monastery in the evenings, unless they'd been kept late.

I suspected the other kids felt a lot like me, though. Meals were the best part of my day. The food wasn't great—far from it, in fact—and the ambience didn't scream four-star restaurant. Heck, the mess tent made the Ptomaine Palace near my dad's university, where they assembled suspicious-smelling subs over the rattraps, look like a classy joint. Here's the thing, though. From the time we dragged ourselves awake to the time our heads hit our dusty pillows, we were constantly starving. We looked forward to getting a tray full of something mostly edible three times a day; plus we had the added bonus of leaving wherever we'd been working in the tomb and seeing our buddies for an hour . . . or a little more, if we stretched it.

You'd think that a real scientific dig would be a little less like high school, but it's not. Cliques sat with cliques. Scientists congregated with scientists. I think my mom and dad envisioned me leaning over an oak table in the candlelight with some Sean Connery–type archaeologist who would impart his brilliance to me over a meal cooked on the campfire. Little did they know that I'd be eating lentils and greasy spinach turnovers on a paper plate while I talked about the same old things with the same types of kids I would have seen in North Seattle High's lunchroom.

"They're such snobs," Sue was saying with a nod over at the next table, where the two conservation team kids sat. For Mallorie's benefit, she added, "*Quelle* stuck-up." With her index finger, she pushed the tip of her nose into the air. Mallorie rolled her eyes and nodded.

"You know, I've had it with them." Bo gave the table a glance and stuck his fork back into what we'd been calling Spamloaf, though we weren't sure it had actual Spam, and it didn't look like a loaf. "I was in the antechamber today. Jan kept dropping her paintbrush or whatever. 'Get that for me?' she kept saying. Like I'd been put on the ground to fetch for her while she and Izumi kept talk-talk-talking. Not! They're not my bosses, no matter how high up they are on those ladders of theirs."

I looked over at the conservation team's table. January James narrowed her eyes when she caught me checking them out. I just smiled back the fakest smile ever to grease my lips until she stood and stalked away in the direction of the food trays. I kept scanning the room. At a table occu-

117

pied only by themselves sat Kathy Klemper and Dag. They were only halfway through their plates. That suited me just fine.

Beneath my top, still knotted on the length of twine I'd tied into a circle around my neck, hung the onyx bracelet from the burial chamber of Tekhen and Tekhnet. Not to be dramatic or anything, but you know those *Lord of the Rings* movies, where the little guy with the hairy feet tries to get rid of a ring that everyone wants while he's being chased around by evil creatures? Well, those Supreme Council guys might not have shared a skeletal hands problem with the movie's faceless guys on big evil horses, but they were just as scary, and a bracelet weighs a ton more than some little old ring.

You know, though, when I thought back on all the times in those films that little Hobbit clutched and clawed at his ring and complained about what a burden it was, I sympathized. The bracelet wasn't exactly fun to have in my possession, either. I constantly worried about someone taking it, or finding it, or banging it up, or breaking it, or any of the hundred things that might completely destroy it and me. At night, when I couldn't sleep because of the log-sawing in the big tent, I thought about the hundreds of ways I might get rid of it.

Here was my chance to take action.

"Excuse me," I said, standing up from my seat.

Connor instantly popped up as well. "Don't go."

I narrowed my eyes at him. "I have to visit the latrine," I told him evenly.

"No, you don't."

"Yes. I do."

The other kids at the table watched us battle back and forth without understanding. Connor, you see, didn't want me to get rid of the bracelet. He didn't think it was a good idea to plant it in Dagmar's possession. "That's, like, so low that it's not even funny as a joke," he had told me when I confided my plan to him the night before.

"I'm still going to do it." I'd already made up my mind. They were never going to do anything about Dag. It was up to me. I was the one who had to do everything, right?

"You could get her in serious trouble," he'd told me.

"That's the idea. Better her than me, right? She deserves it."

"How are you going to feel when they arrest her?" he had asked me.

Connor had sounded so much like one of my parents right then, posing it as an ethical dilemma so I'd cave in and do what he wanted, that for the first time he irritated me. "Good," I said. When I'd seen his disappointment, I had softened my answer. "They're not going to arrest her. They'll just question her and take the bracelet to the relics trailer for photographs, never to be seen again. She'll think up an excuse!"

"But what if she is arrested? What if they take her away and the rest of us have to go home because we don't have a chaperone?"

I'd scoffed. "They wouldn't do that."

"They might."

"They won't."

"They might."

It had been quite the standoff. Connor hadn't been totally upset with me, but I could tell he didn't like the idea. "I'll think about it, then," I had told him in the tent. I'd thought about it until I was convinced I was right.

Now we were facing off across the table from each other again. "Can't you hold it in?" he asked me.

"Dude!" said Bo, appalled.

"I've thought it over," I said significantly, "and I think it's best if I don't."

"Did you *really* think it over?"

He was upsetting me on a few levels. For one thing, hadn't he been telling me just yesterday that this camp was better for having me around? Had he been lying, or what? Then there was the issue of his tone. Connor Marsh was definitely *not* my father. Third . . . well, third, he was drawing a lot of attention to both of us, and that was exactly what I did not need. Maybe that had been his intention. I sat back down. "Yes, as a matter of fact, I thought it over for quite a long time."

He sat as well. "And?"

"And I still want to . . ." I looked around the table, where four other sets of eyes watched us with full attention. "I still intend to go to the latrine."

When I stood on my feet once more, he followed suit. "Then I'm going with you."

"Dude!" Bo said again.

"Connor, I really think that she can go to the latrine by *herself,*" Deidre said.

"Thanks, Dee," I told her, swinging my leg over the bench. "I'll be back in a few."

I hated walking away from the table with Connor in that mood, though. I hated arguing with him. How in the world was the worst going to happen to Dag? I wasn't planning on calling the Supreme Council and turning her in. I just wanted to put the bracelet into her backpack and get rid of it. She'd probably just hand it over to one of the archaeologists and not get into a lick of trouble, right? Connor worried too much. He'd see, once I took care of this matter, that Chloe knew best—just like I'd known best with the shower incident. We'd all gotten clean clothes out of that one, hadn't we?

I stepped out of the mess tent into the auxiliary tent, where everyone could dump their bags and rinse their hands with a disinfecting alcohol scrub before every meal. "Going somewhere?" someone said to me.

I almost jumped right out of my nearly fresh-smelling skin. Seth Tousson had loomed up out of nowhere. He stood before me, a sight in black jeans and leather, the neck of his tank top scooping low enough to reveal the line of definition between his pecs. His long hair was tied into a braid tonight. He tilted his neck when I leaped back. "Man, you look like you're seeing a ghost."

"Maybe I am," I said, when my heartbeat settled down to something less than a machine-gun rate. "It's not like you've been around much lately." In fact, I hadn't seen much of Seth since he'd tumbled off that rope ladder six days before. The graze on his head was still a little on the scabby side, but looking much better. "I thought you were avoiding me."

"Nah! Well, maybe a little," he admitted.

He didn't seem to want to say anything more. Nor did he seem to want to leave. "I see your bulldog got your leather jacket back to you," I finally said.

Seth looked down at the floor. "I wish you wouldn't call Jan names like that, Chloe. She's a nice girl."

"Which makes me . . . ?"

"You're fishing for compliments." Seth seemed uncertain whether I was teasing or being serious. I'm not sure I knew, either. "For the record, I didn't send her to get the jacket. That was entirely her own idea. I don't know if you know, but Jan and I are . . ." He grinned sheepishly rather than finishing the sentence.

"Oh." Oh, indeed. That explained a lot. No wonder January had been so nasty to me that night in the tent. "Did she think that you and I . . . Oh." If she'd been under the impression that Seth and I were an item, or that I was trying to start something with Seth, that would explain her rudeness to Connor as well.

"She might have thought that you were, you know . . . stuck on me. That's kind of why I wanted to talk to you that night, to make sure you didn't think that just because we'd had a quick peck . . ."

What did Jan think I was, some kind of prowling mantrap, out to snare every guy I got my hands on? Running up against another weird perception of me was just too much to handle right now.

And a quick peck? I didn't think so. That had been a genuine, honest-to-God, solicited kiss Seth had given me in the antechamber of the tomb last week. You know, though, I didn't mind him rewriting history. Sometimes people needed to do that for themselves. Trust me—I knew that better than anyone. "Yeah," I said, interrupting him. "I mean, jeez, it wasn't that great a kiss anyway, right?" That might have been a little mean of me, but frankly, I was in a hurry to get him the heck out of the room.

"Right," he said uneasily. "Wait. It wasn't?"

"So you'd better go on in to see her," I told him. "Sounds like she might be the jealous type, if you know what I mean. And I don't think you want her to catch you with Chloe the Heartbreaker, right?"

There was a laugh if I'd ever heard one. That didn't mean, however, that I'd actually *wanted* him to laugh. I waited with my lips pressed together while he got over his amusement, then smiled more falsely than I had with Jan only a few minutes ago. "You're a good kid," he said at last.

"You'd better go in to dinner before I get the urge to drag you off to some other tomb and push you down a burial shaft again," I teased, anxious for him to go. "I've got to get to the latrine, anyway," I said. To get the point across, I squeezed my knees together and jumped up and down a little.

"Okay." He winked at me. "You'd better hurry."

"Yeah. And don't be such a stranger!" I yelled at his back. I didn't entertain any illusions about Seth and I being great pals in the future, but at the same time I didn't like the notion that he might be tiptoeing around me.

Once he was gone, I could relax from my posture of fake urinary distress. What happened next was simple enough that when I replayed it over and over again in my head for the following twenty-four hours, I could remember every detail:

1) I ran over to the area where all us kids threw our backpacks before dinner. Dag had marked off a corner of the tent with an orange flag with the Dig Egypt! logo on it, and we all knew our lives would be worthless if our packs were found anywhere else.

2) I spotted Dag's bag in the center of the mess, identifiable by the tiniest patch of blue on one of its pockets. I didn't have to pull it out of the stack to know that would be her Swedish flag.

3) I opened the outermost pocket of the pack.

4) I removed the bracelet from around my neck and slipped off the twine knot holding it. The little lapis

bird with the beady eyes seemed to stare at me when I gave it a last look.

5) I slipped the bracelet into the pack and zipped it tight.

Then I went back into the mess tent.

"Took you long enough," said Sue when I sat back down. "We almost ate the rest of your lentils."

"You can have them." I shoved them over. Sue instantly began dividing the rest of the soggy miniature bean Frisbees between her plate and Mallorie's.

For once I really wasn't hungry. My escapade had left me feeling slightly nauseated. And there was the matter of Connor. His glare would have made me sick to my stomach even if I'd had a hearty appetite. I couldn't stand the sight of his disappointment.

"So you did it?" he asked me over the table, not bothering to keep his voice down.

"Yes, I did." I tried to stay calm.

"And?"

"Duuuude!" Bo protested. "We don't need the details!"

"And it was fine," I told him. "Just fine."

"Oh, man." Bo pushed away the last of his dinner. "TMI."

"I'm done too," I announced. "I'm going back to my tent."

"So am I." If grabbing a tray with attitude was an Olympic sport, Connor would have won the gold.

Not to be outdone, I grabbed mine as well. We both stalked to the waste bins, disposed of our trays in utter silence, and began our walk back to the tents. Our walk, did I say? Hardly. We'd taken walks together before where we were a pair. We'd been friendly then—we'd held hands and talked and kissed and nuzzled and all sorts of stuff. Now, though, we were just two people who happened to be walking to the same destination at roughly the same time.

It hurt.

What was I supposed to do, with him so close but saying nothing? What did he expect from me, some kind of apology? Did he want me to say I was wrong, that I shouldn't have done it? Was this going to be one of those things I could never make up, no matter how hard I tried? Did I want to try? With every step seemed to come a new question.

What path did I have to follow for some answers, huh?

I was startled out of my thoughts when he spoke up right as we reached the camp. "I hope at least you didn't let anyone see you."

"Of course not." I sounded angrier than I intended; I softened my volume. "Seth caught me in the outer tent, but I pretended I had to pee."

"Oh. Seth."

"Yeah, Seth. Who thinks I'm a kid, and who was all concerned that I'd lose my heart to any guy who kisses me."

"And I guess you never lose your heart," he said.

I whirled around and threw my hands up in the air. "Exactly how many different arguments are we having here?" I asked him, truly angry. "Anything else you want to throw into the pot? It's argument gumbo, folks. Just toss it all in!" When I saw his face, my heart fell. I really had distressed him with my little outburst. "I think we should have only one fight at a time, that's all. Don't bring Seth into this. I don't give a flying fig about Seth. Don't bring you and me into this. I . . . I like you a lot," I confessed to him. "You know I do. I'm mad at you right now, like you're mad at me, but that doesn't change the fact that I like you better than I like just about anyone else."

"Chloe—I'm sorry."

"And I'm sorry that you aren't on board with me," I told him. "I'm sorry we're having this stupid fight. But I don't . . ." Oh, it was frustrating, not to have the right words to say! "I honestly don't know what else I could have done, Connor."

"I think you should have . . . I think you could have gone and told someone what happened. Dr. Battista would have understood."

"Would you have done it?" I asked him. "If I'd given you the bracelet, would you have gone to Dr. Battista and said, 'Hey, I found this in the tombs and accidentally took it away and kept it for a week, but here, it's yours now'? Would you really?" After a minute, he shook his head. "No, you wouldn't. Because you've got some funky secret that you won't share and you're afraid to get into trouble. I've already got two stupid, *stupid* warnings. You honestly think confessing wouldn't have gotten me a third?"

"You're not a dishonest person, though," he said, shaking his head.

I thought about that one. Wasn't I? Wasn't this entire trip dishonest? "I don't know what to tell you," I finally answered. "I don't think there's anything I can say."

"Me neither."

There we were, back to silence again. And I still didn't have an answer to even one of my questions.

"I'll leave you alone." I turned to enter my tent.

"Chloe." When I looked over my shoulder, he had removed his baseball cap and was running his hands through his curls. "I . . . the way I feel about you . . ." My heart seemed to skip several lifetimes' worth of beats in the seconds that followed. "I just . . ." He put his cap back on

126

again. "Let's try to talk about all this mess tomorrow, maybe."

"Yeah." I felt hollow inside.

"Good night."

If I'd been back at home, I could have indulged myself in a fine sulk. I could have grabbed a box of chocolate milk from the fridge and a bag of pretzels from the cupboard, and sneaked them up to my room, where I could have turned on the radio, loud. I could have stuffed my face with snapped pretzel halves and washed them down with the chocolate milk, letting the sweet and salty tastes soothe me. I could have made little voodoo paper dolls with Kathy Klemper's face on them, or Dag's, or Jan's, or even Connor's. I could have put on my mix CD of "Life Is Sucky and Then You Die" songs, and dived under my sheets. They would have been crisp and clean and smelled of fabric softener.

I felt a sharp pang of homesickness. It hit me in the chest like a hammer, all at once. If I'd been home I would have been good and miserable and sorry for myself with all the trimmings. Here in the desert, the only thing I could do was throw myself onto my cot with my back to the opening.

You know, cots really just aren't cozy, even when you've got your blanket lining the bottom. I flopped over and tried to find a comfortable position, finally grabbing my pillow and flipping it over into a new position beneath my neck. It was right then that my head banged down on something hard. And round.

I pulled the object from my pillowcase and held it in my palm. So thunderstruck was I that I bolted to my feet. Right at that moment I badly wished I'd made that latrine pit stop, because the pee I'd been pretending to hold in earlier now suddenly wanted to come spraying out. "*Connor!*" I yelled at the top of my voice.

He came running. I knew he would. He ripped back the tent flap, wide-eyed, out of breath, and carrying a flashlight in his hand like a bludgeon. "Are you okay?" he exclaimed. "Oh, my God, I thought you were in trouble. I couldn't have stood it if you'd been— Are you okay? What's the matter?"

"Look!"

He stared at the object in my hands. "I thought you—"

"I did!"

"Then Dag—"

"She couldn't!" I started to tremble. "It's impossible! She was in the mess tent when we left!"

In my hand I held the bracelet. The very same bracelet I'd hidden in Dag's backpack only a few minutes before. The bracelet I had found under my pillow just then. Connor and I stared at each other in disbelief over its black sheen. Before I realized what was happening, I found myself sitting down heavily on the dirt floor.

Something seriously freaky was going on here.

Nine

"Do you believe in curses?"

I thought I could predict Dr. Battista's reply to my question. In fact, I specifically asked her because I wanted someone cool, confident, and thoroughly scientific to say, *Chloe, don't be silly. You know there's no such thing as curses. Why, you'll be believing in the tooth fairy and leprechauns next.*

I really didn't want to believe in leprechauns. I don't even *like* Lucky Charms cereal.

Dr. Battista, though, raised her head from the row of hieroglyphics we were uncovering with small brushes and surprised me. "Yes, I do," she said quite matter-of-factly. I felt as though she'd just announced that she believed little colored gummy marshmallows and nasty sugared lumps of grain could be magically delicious. "Curses are part and parcel of my heritage."

The mummies of Tekhen and Tekhnet had been carefully wrapped three days before and sent to Cairo for X-rays and studies. It was impossible for them to remain in the tomb while we tried to excavate. For thousands of years they had been shut away under airtight stone. Moisture was their enemy, and we exposed them to it with every breath, every syllable we spoke. Until the tomb's excavation and restoration were complete, the sisters would stay in a barium chamber in Cairo.

Dr. Battista had overseen the transfer herself, insulating the delicate remains as gently as she might handle a baby. One by one they had been lifted up to the surface on stretchers; most of the Egyptian workers gathered around at the top of the burial shaft and carefully surrounded the stretchers. Heads hung, their voices singing a doleful, low tune I didn't understand, they had marched up the slanting stone stairs carrying the twin mummies between them. Dr. Battista and Eddie and I followed.

It was weird; I'd felt like we were the primary mourners at a funeral. As we had passed from the stairwell into the vestibule, all activity stopped. The archaeologists and the Dig Egypt! kids, regardless of what team they were on, put down their trowels and brushes and marking pens and cameras and rose to their feet. Some of them had clasped their hands in respect. Just about everyone lowered their heads. Nothing had been planned. It had just happened. After Tekhen and Tekhnet had been escorted outside, where they had been loaded onto a truck that would take them to a helicopter farther out, Connor had come over and put his hand on my shoulder. I had liked that gesture. Remembering it now, I wondered if I'd ever feel it again.

With the mummies gone, Dr. Battista and I had spent most of the week clearing flood debris from the bases of the sarcophagi, working on small stools next to each other, occasionally stopping to transcribe the inscriptions we found. It was quiet work, and I enjoyed it.

Yet we hadn't talked much. Not about anything beyond the pictographs underneath our fingertips, anyway. The comment about her heritage had been the first personal thing she'd said to me in quite some time. "I had heard," I said carefully, wondering if what I was about to say might be remotely offensive, "that your grandmother was a gypsy?"

Dr. Battista sat back. In the light of the utility bulb, the creases of her face took on shadows that made her look older than she was. At the same time, though, with her thin hands and arms and her thick hair pulled back into a ponytail, she looked like a young girl. "My mother's family was Romany," she said. "Gypsy."

"Oh." There was more I wanted to ask, but I was afraid to open my mouth. This sounded like something private. *Wait a minute, though,* I thought. My mother's family was Scottish, and there was nothing particularly private about that. Why should being gypsy—Romany—be any different? "And they believed in curses?"

"Oh, very much so. Evil eyes. Hexes. Amulets, talismans, the warding off of ill spirits. All of it nonsense, of course."

Okay. Now she'd confused me. "But I thought you just said . . ."

She let her head loll back, then slowly rotated it around, as if trying to relax her neck muscles. "Those kinds of curses are fictitious. They're a bit of mystery my mother's people cultivated so they could pass unmolested through the countryside. Superstitious peasants are always willing to believe the worst about those who live on the fringes of a society, like the Romany." She set down her instruments and held her knee in her hands, as if she were about to tell me a story. "But I do believe many people walk this earth cursed."

"Okay. How?"

"It's unfashionable for a scientist to believe in a supreme

being," said Dr. Battista. Her dark eyes glinted as she looked at me. "And even more unfashionable for her to admit it. But I do. Sometimes I think I believe in God, or at least in the call of a higher power. Sometimes I think it's more of an organic force that determines our fates—the spirit of the world working through us. Most of the time I don't think it matters. I think the call drives us, though, to strive to learn, or to be creative. To be more than just passive consumers of frozen dinners and watchers of television." I nodded. I could understand what she was getting at. It didn't sound exactly like what my Methodist parents believed, but I had the feeling that if Dr. Battista and my college-résumé-obsessed parents ever met, they would approve of each other.

"There's a race of men and women, though, who don't hear the call. They ignore it. They deafen their ears to it. They spend their waking days living in fear of progress. They fear change. They fear outsiders and strangers and shut them out of their lives. Once these people have shut their ears and hearts to the call, they are cursed for life."

"You really believe that?" It sounded crazy to me. I mean, I understood what she meant about people who seemed to shut themselves away from new things, hating change. I guess I was a little like that myself. Until now I hadn't thought of myself as cursed, though.

She nodded. "And when one or more of these people come into much power, they will not use it for progress, but for destruction." Dr. Battista reached out with a finger to touch the basalt of the sarcophagus. It was a solemn moment. I kept quiet. "My grandmother and her sisters, her brothers, and her children were taken with other Romany to the concentration camps in Czechoslovakia during World

War Two. Most died there, because of these cursed men. My mother did not."

I shivered. Listening to her grim story in a completely dark tomb fifty feet under the earth only makes it ten times as ominous. "So." Dr. Battista picked up her brushes again. "As my mother used to tell me, and as her mother told her before that, never allow yourself to settle and become complacent. Always keep moving, and listening, and seeing." She went back to work.

I didn't know what to say. *I'm sorry* simply wouldn't cut it. I didn't think I had to say anything. After a few moments, though, I spoke up. "Thank you."

"You are welcome. Did I answer your question?"

To admit otherwise would sound stupid. "Yes. It's just that Dag . . . I mean, Ms. Sorensson . . . is always going on about mummy curses."

She sat back again and stared at me. "Don't tell me you believe in *that* nonsense."

"No!" Was I lying? I didn't know. What else could account for the bracelet's sudden reappearance under my pillow the night before?

Connor and I had talked over basically every possibility. Could Dag have been the one to do it? Sure! If she owned a magic watch that stopped time and let her zoom from the mess tent to her backpack to the big tent and back to her dinner tray again, that is. The other kids had sworn up and down, when I questioned them discreetly, that Dag never left her table.

My other suspect was Connor. He had the motivation. He'd never wanted me to plant the bracelet in Dag's pack to begin with. It would be just like him to try to rescue me from myself, I pointed out to him.

"I'd need the same magic watch," he'd told me. "And what about you? Maybe you did it yourself."

"Are you *crazy?*"

Was I? Could I have imagined my felonious little act? Had the bracelet caught on my pants and I'd somehow . . . Oh, that was stupid. I *remembered* everything about what I'd done.

The only other possibility was that someone had seen me do it. Someone had been lurking in that tent, watching me, and when I went back into the mess tent, they'd unzipped Dag's backpack, retrieved the bracelet, and raced across the camp to stash it under my pillow.

Who in the world, though, would have even *known* to do such a thing? That was what bothered me. I didn't tell anyone except Connor that I'd found that bracelet. Only Connor knew that I was going to try to fob it off onto Dag. Could I have put it in the wrong backpack? Maybe, but I couldn't think of anyone else with a blue patch on the pocket. Besides, who at camp would *know* that returning the bracelet to my cot would drive me absolutely bonkers? And instantaneously, too?

Can you see why I was beginning to wonder about the mummy's curse?

"Dagmar is a fool—and I will appreciate your not repeating those words to anyone. She does not think with a critical mind, obviously. The superstitious will do that. They will ignore the evidence of the eyes and the powers of the brain and accept any magical explanation that occurs to them, no matter how illogical." As if that were that, Dr. Battista leaned forward and started to work again, instructing me to remove some of the rougher accumulations before she tackled them with her own tools.

Hmmm. Leaping to illogical explanations sounded like

what I was doing. There had to be a solution to the Mystery of the Mummy's Bracelet. One thing, though: I was no Nancy Drew, and I didn't have a clue what it might be.

My dad's a pretty dull kind of guy who just teaches his classes during the day and spends his nights reading and working on lecture notes and papers, but my mom works for a business where they're all the time telling each other to "think outside the box." She says it at home a lot, whenever she's trying to get me or my brothers or my dad to be creative. As in, *Don't tell me you can't figure out a topic for your paper. Think outside the box!* The heck! I've always wondered what that box looked like. Was it big, like a refrigerator box? More like a shoe box? Why a box? Why not "think outside the bag of Fritos" or in my brothers' case, "think outside the *Sports Illustrated*"?

I knew what she meant, though. I couldn't just let the same ideas bounce around and around in my head. I had only three possible solutions, and I'd revisited them so many times it felt I knew them better than my own name. Those same old patterns of thinking weren't getting me anywhere.

I needed to abandon the ways I'd been thinking and look for another answer. All the rest of that morning I paid attention to my work and gave the paranoid portions of my brain a rest.

Finally Dr. Battista noticed the time and let me off for lunch. Connor waited for me outside the entrance to the tomb. To tell the truth, I was surprised to see him there. We hadn't touched again on what had happened between us the night before. I guess I was kind of assuming we'd broken up.

But you know, is it possible to break up something that hasn't even really begun? Don't get me wrong; I enjoyed every single minute I spent with Connor. I liked talking to him. I really loved when we would stand or sit close to each other and . . . well, you know. Not talk. Unlike with Seth, where kissing had felt more like a science lab experiment, with Connor I thought that maybe things could maybe grow into . . . I don't know. Let me put it this way: I was happier when I imagined my life with Connor in it.

But oy! All this pressure on my poor little brain! I needed a vacation from both Chloes—the brave one *and* the coward.

"Hey," Connor said to me.

"Hey," I said back.

"Are we talking today?"

"The heck! You're doing it again," I told him. When he looked surprised, I explained. "Who said anything about not talking? We were never not talking. We were talking last night about a lot of stuff, but we never talked about not talking."

"Okay, okay," he said. "I feel like my brain is covered with as much dirt and crud as the rest of me, so before you say the words *not talking* again and make it explode, let's just call a truce?"

"Do I want to call a truce with you?" I asked, doubtful.

"Yeah, you do."

"Why?"

"Here's why."

He reached out, cupped my chin with his hand, and pulled me toward him. When our lips met, it felt as if we hadn't argued at all. He pulled me closer so that our bodies complemented each other, as if they'd been made to fit. One of his arms wrapped around my shoulder blades. The other one . . . Was his hand on my butt? His hand was on my butt! Weirder still, I kind of liked it. While we continued to kiss, I lowered my own right hand until it went south of the belt border and stretched across his own backside. He didn't object to that at all, either. I gave it a squeeze.

"Man, Chloe! Gross! Get a *room!*"

"*Ooh-la-la!*" Mallorie actually winked at us.

"You know," I told Sue, "that was the first sentence from Mallorie's mouth that I actually understood."

"*Elle vous a compris,*" Sue told Mallorie, and then said to me, "But I repeat. Get a room already!"

"We were just . . ." Connor coughed as he separated from me.

"Yes, we were just . . ."

"Yeah," Sunita said in a sarcastic voice, hands on her hips. "I don't have a clue what you were *really* doing because where I come from, kids only hold hands until we're twenty-seven and get married. Then our babies appear in a cabbage patch. Hello! I'm from L.A.! We *invented* French-kissing. Or maybe Mallorie's country did. Either way, guys, we all know what you've been doing during your *walks* at night."

I don't know whether Mallorie had picked up enough English to understand Sunita's speech, or whether she was just picking up on the general playful mood, but she suddenly started making a cartoon kissy face, lips protruding out like a blowfish. *"Ah, je t'aime! Embrasse-moi! Embrasse-moi!"*

Somehow I managed to reach down past all the embarrassment and mortification inside and pull up a snort. "Whatever," I told both of them. I couldn't help but smile a little. When I tried to reach up and conceal my amusement, I found my nose and lips and chin absolutely covered with grit. My forehead, too. I shook my head and a rain of soot fell down. I was filthy! How in the world could Connor even stand to touch me like this?

Maybe he really did like me after all.

As if reading my mind, Connor grinned at me.

"All right," I told him. "Truce."

"See?" He swaggered a little. "I told you you'd come around."

"Me!" I was only pretending to be outraged. Even though I knew we still had issues to resolve, it felt good to be back on familiar ground. Once again, I felt as if I had hope.

None of us was walking too quickly up the slope to the camp as we chattered and gossiped about the day's events, so it wasn't surprising when we were overtaken near the end of our trek. "Excuse us," I heard someone say.

"Yes, pardon us," said another voice.

January James and Izumi Shikibu. Absolutely fan-freakin'-tastic. Because you know, I really needed to have the first good mood of my long morning spoiled by coming into contact with the conservation team. They simply brushed by without saying another word. Although neither of them came within as close as an arm's length, after they passed, Jan looked over her shoulder at me. She tugged her neckline, tossed her hair, and cinched her upper lip into a sneer.

Ooooooo. I couldn't *stand* Jan. And she and Seth were close? More power to her, I guess, but I really didn't have a clue what Seth saw in her. It wasn't personality, that's for sure. Smarts? How much brainpower did it take to copy hieroglyphics? Was it her breasts? Was Seth shallow enough to want someone for her cup size?

I was reapplying my lip gloss when Sue spoke up. "They are *so* rude."

"Don't let it bother you," Connor suggested.

"But it does," Sue grumbled. "You know, yesterday when Mallorie and Bo and I were walking back to our

tents après dinner, we ran into Jan, and when I said *bon-jour!* she was *très* rude and acted like I hadn't said boo."
I only half listened to the story. Sue was always complaining about Jan and Izumi. "So I said, like this, 'Hel-*lo*, Jan!' and she jumped like I'd stabbed her with a sword. *Une épée.*"

"That's pretty typical," I said, wondering what we were going to have for lunch. A dozen yards ahead, Jan and Izumi turned the corner up the path to the mess tent. Just before they vanished completely, Jan turned around again and looked directly at me. She said something to her friend and shook her head.

That's when it struck me. Forget about thinking outside the box. I felt like someone had taken the box—one of those metal jobbies with a combination lock on the front—brought it down on top of my head, and sent me crashing to my knees. "You passed her after dinner?" I repeated back to Sue as I brought the entire group to a halt.

"Yeah. Oh, and today in the antechamber, she—"
I didn't care what Jan had done in the antechamber. "She passed her after dinner," I said to Connor. He didn't catch the significance at first. "After *dinner*," I repeated.

His jaw dropped slightly open. Good. He'd finally understood. "You passed her after dinner?" he asked Sue.

"Are you guys like, on something?" she answered. "Or is there dust in your ears? Earwax? What?"

"Where was she coming from?" I had to know.

"From the direction of camp. Why?"

"Yes!" Some part of my memory recalled seeing Jan get up last night after I'd smiled at her from my own table. It was entirely possible that she'd seen me leave the mess tent shortly afterward. If she'd followed me, which sounded just like the suspicious and nasty kind of thing a suspicious and nasty-minded person might do, she would have seen me talking to Seth.

And Jan was obviously sooooooo jealous of my coming anywhere near Seth that she'd try anything to freak me out. She'd been the one to dive into Dagmar's bag, grab the bracelet, and hide it in my tent. Suddenly everything made perfect sense! I *was* Nancy Drew, baby!

I was so filled with sudden glee that I reached out and grabbed Connor's hand. We jumped up in the air together several times, just like we were kids. "She was coming back from the camp!"

"How awesome is that?" Connor seemed just as excited as I was. "She was coming back from the camp!"

Sue and Mallorie looked at both of us as if we were fresh off the funny farm. "Okay. Whatever. You guys *are* on something. *Allons,* Mallorie. I want to change clothes."

We waited until they'd left us before celebrating some more. "It's perfect!" I crowed. "She's got everything. Opportunity, motive, bad fashion sense . . ."

"What are you going to do?"

I thought that one over for a minute. What did I want? Revenge, pretty much. She and Izumi had probably been cackling over their little joke all day. Oh, yeah, real funny, guys. Who was going to have the last laugh, though? That's right. Chloe. Queen of Denial. Only this time the only thing that was going to be denied was their sick and twisted fun. "I've got to get to the mess tent," I finally decided.

"Wait."

"You don't understand. I've got to get there *now.*" I didn't know why I had a sense of sure urgency deep in my gut. I simply knew I had to confront Jan as soon as possible.

"I'm not convinced."

He didn't have to grab my wrist or tug at my shirt. He

only needed to say those three simple words to make me stop in my tracks. "Hold on. A minute ago you were doing the Snoopy dance with me. Are you getting a conscience again?"

He closed his eyes at that remark. I felt a little bad—I would have been peeved at me too. When he opened them again, he spoke with patient, even words. "One thing I don't get. Why in the world would she go to all the trouble to return the artifact to you? I mean, if she's jealous of you and Seth, why not just push you up against the wall and, you know, rough you up a little?"

Part of me warmed at the way he spit out Seth's name, as if it tasted bad in his mouth. Was he a little jealous himself? "Think outside the box," I told him, while I searched for an answer myself.

"What? Chloe, listen, I know you're all about action and not so much about thinking—"

"What's that supposed to mean?" I asked, seriously annoyed.

"It's not the way it sounds! Listen, whenever I'm about to do something risky I hear this little voice in my head. It says, 'Hey you, be careful. That might be dangerous.' " I stared at him. Oh, yeah, I knew that voice. "You do so many crazy things that I've got to wonder if you ever listen to it."

I ignored what he was saying. Of all the people in the world, he didn't have to lecture me about holding back. "I know!" Inspiration had struck me. Something had happened that night in the tent. It was on the tip of my tongue. "Jan was in the tent. She asked for the jacket . . . and after I fetched it from under the bed, I went through the pockets. That's when I found the bracelet again. She must have seen it! Connor, she had to have seen it! Oh, I'm going to get her so good."

My realization made him grab my wrist. "Chloe—"

My skin burned when I yanked my arm out of his grip. "I hear the voice. Connor, I hear that voice all the time. It's the voice that's kept me from doing *anything* with my life. If you want to act all timid because you're scared of going home, fine. Be that way. But I, for once in my life, refuse to be a coward."

"When have *you* ever been a coward?" He sounded so amazed at the idea that for a moment I was overjoyed. I really had pulled it off, hadn't I? I'd done such a good job of hoodwinking everyone that I'd fooled even the smartest boy here. The feeling faded instantly, though.

"All my freakin' life." A few of the Egyptians were walking by right then, talking to each other in Arabic. I lowered my voice to a growl. "Every single day of my sad and sorry life until I got here. Until Egypt you know what kind of person I was? Think of how scared Deidre is on her best day and multiply the annoyance level by about a hundred. Back home I don't hang with Baz Wilder. Connor, if I'd ever tried to talk to Baz or any of his group, my stomach would flip so much that I'd do a Linda Blair routine from *The Exorcist* with green vomit all over the place. You know why you couldn't quite place me on the first day? It's because I'm one of those pathetic people with a pathetic life that no one ever pays attention to." My anger was so overwhelming that I didn't dare look at his expression.

"No one here thinks you're pathetic," he whispered. "I don't."

"That's because I've been faking it. I've faked it since day one. You want to know what I do? I clench my teeth and *endure,* because whatever's going to happen here is going to happen, whether I like it or not. I *endure,* and eventually it'll be over and I can go on with my sorry and pathetic life.

And little by little it gets easier." I blinked at my words. I was right. It had gotten easier. How many times in the last two weeks had I without a thought climbed up and down a rope ladder that once terrified me? How close had I stood to the mummies without trembling, the day Dr. Battista wrapped them up?

I didn't break my stride, though. "I know exactly what you're thinking now," I told him. I'd had enough experience with my family's disgust at the Queen of Denial to recognize it. "You're finally realizing that I don't even want to be here. That I'm a fake. That I'm not brave enough. That I'm not like you, and never was."

The pause that followed my words was so long that I began to think of turning and walking away. Finally he spoke in words that were slow and soft and sad. "All that stuff about you being a coward?" he finally said. "That's all in your head, Chloe. It sounds to me like you worry and worry about not being brave enough . . . but brave enough for what? You were brave enough to come here. You're brave enough to be a leader day after day. My God, you're brave enough to do a hundred impossible things before breakfast without blinking. I don't care what stupid, self-defeating thoughts are in your brain. I can't get inside your head. I can only know you by what you do and say."

Connor made me want to cry. I bit my lips, focusing on the berry flavor to keep tears from welling up as he continued speaking.

"If you're too busy *enduring* things, though, I think you're denying yourself the chance to really enjoy them." Yes, I'd known that truth the moment I'd stood beside him on the cliff, when he made me feel as if I hadn't really seen the desert at all until then. Enduring things made them flat and lifeless. "Was I something you only endured?"

"No." I looked him in his eyes then. Did I see hope there? "Never."

"For the record, you're not a coward," he said. "Not here in Egypt. Not to me."

When he tried to take my hands, I slipped them away. I didn't want to, but I couldn't accept his tenderness right then. I felt raw and exposed, bruised all over in the deep purples and blues of an Egyptian sunset. And talk about confused! I wanted to run. I wanted to stay. I wanted to stay and run in place. It was all I could do to keep from crying from shame and laughing with relief at the same time. Was I screwed up, or what?

"Okay," I sniffled at last. "Thanks." How inadequate that sounded!

"You really are great," he told me. "I think you've needed to be here even more than I did." He was being kind. Why was he being so kind?

"I need to . . . I need to leave."

He grinned a little. "You're still going to go after Jan, aren't you?"

Strangely, I didn't detect any signs of an impending lecture in his words. "Yeah. I am. You think I shouldn't?"

His grin popped open to let out laughter. "It sounds like you've got a louder little voice in your head than I do. You don't need me trying to tell you what to do." I reached for his hands, hoping I could make up for not accepting them a moment before. "But, hey, Chloe."

"What?" I asked.

"Be careful. Promise?"

I nodded. I wasn't looking for my third and final reprimand. Funny—for weeks I'd been thinking that I didn't want to be here in Egypt. Now I couldn't stand the idea of being forced to leave.

"You know what?" I told him after that realization. He raised his eyebrows so high that they scraped the strap on his backward-facing baseball cap. "I'm not scared of Jan. I'm not scared at all right now."

"Told you so," he said. He was right. He had. "You'll be careful?"

Careful? Of course I would. I'd promised, right?

Ten

"Hiiiiiiii, Izumi!"

Everyone has a certain kind of girl in their high school who's nicely dressed and carefully coiffed. Her makeup's applied according to the latest recommendations in the teen magazines. She's bubbly and fake as all get-out. She's the kind of girl who flocks with others just like her and giggles at anyone who's different. Right at that moment, I was trying to be that kind of girl. Okay, so I was failing miserably on the dress and hair fronts, and I stank like a potato straight out of the sack, but at least I had the voice right. Three parts sugar, one part plastic.

When I eased onto the bench next to Izumi, I cast an eye across the mess tent. I'd timed my swoop to coincide with Jan's absence. Apparently she'd forgotten her silverware or something. A moment before, after I'd set down my tray on the far side of the enclosure and then pretended to be going back to the line for something to drink, she'd risen and stalked around the edge of the tent in the direction of the food line.

This was my big chance. "You know, I've been meaning to tell you that you are always *so* pretty. Are you wearing scent? What is it?" With a great deal of casualness I draped my hand over Jan's food tray.

Izumi really did have an air of sophistication around her. Great complexion. Flawless skin. Beautiful hair. She reminded me of what Sunita might be like in two years, once she got back to a regular schedule of bathing. You know how there are certain kids who just seem ready to be full-fledged adults? They're confident and ready to shuck the cocoon and fly away to better things. Izumi was one of those girls just starting to stretch out those butterfly wings. "Aren't you sweet!" she said, peering at me like she couldn't quite remember my name. She sniffed at her wrist, as if hoping to find traces of whatever perfume she'd spritzed on that morning.

"I didn't want to bug you, but I just *had* to say it," I said, letting my hand drop to my lap. "You really are the most glamorous girl in Dig Egypt!" Where was Jan? For some reason a flock of German tourists were milling around the tent carrying lunch trays, making it difficult to see anything from my seated position.

"Oh! Thank you!"

"No problem!" I told her. "Not at all!"

No problem for me, anyway. Jan, though—now, she was going to get the problem surprise of her life when she lifted up the napkin on her tray. But you know, mess with Chloe Bryce and you'll only end up regretting it.

I'd hoped to make a clean getaway, but I found it difficult to navigate back to my table when so many of the Germans were taking their sweet time to settle down. What if Jan caught me nearby? Well, she'd find out soon enough anyway that I'd been there.

Sue and the others had just gotten their plates by the time I got back to the far side of the tent. "I guess someone didn't bother to change her clothes," said Sue, looking at me. "*Quelle* filthy!"

"I was hungry," I explained.

"I suppose so!"

"How come we have to sit so close to the tent opening?" Deidre wanted to know. "Sand gets in my food when we're this close to the door. And there might be snakes."

"Yeah, way to go on the choice of tables, Chloe," said Bo. "Not. Hey, are any of you guys going to the slide show tonight?"

"What slide show?" asked Deidre.

"Some lecture by some guy about something." Despite all their complaining, the four of them began digging into their food with gusto, chattering about what they should do that night. I was too busy looking for Jan to pay much attention. It wasn't until I spotted her red hair and freckles through the mob that I relaxed a little.

"Aren't you going to eat?" Bo looked ready to spear my spinach turnover with his fork.

"Hands off, Hoover," I joked. That kid had one notorious appetite. "Yeah, yeah, I'm eating. Sheesh." I twisted open the cap of my Coke bottle and set it to the side of my plate, and went to pick up my napkin. "Everything actually kind of looks good today, doesn't it? Shawarma, turnovers . . ."

I froze. A heavy object lay inside my napkin. I'd assumed it was my fork or knife, but when I'd lifted it up, something toppled out of it and into my lap.

Something black.

Something round.

Something with a lapis bird projecting out of it in the middle.

Moments before I'd been feeling confident and even cocky; now I felt sick to my stomach again. I looked up. The

German mob had separated in the middle, as if invisible hands had pushed them apart. Across the tent, I saw Jan toss her hair back and *glare* in my direction.

I tried to smile like nothing was wrong. It wasn't supposed to have worked this way. *Jan* was supposed to be the one writhing in torment right now. Not me! I was so stunned that my lips twisted and curled in places they shouldn't have. I probably looked as if I were working up a really good entry for the international World's Freakiest Face contest.

Once again I stared at the bracelet in my lap. It was *impossible* that I had it. How had it happened? *How?*

"Chloe?" Sue was staring at me with her eyebrows raised. "Is something bugging you?" If only she knew! I shook my head, but she wasn't satisfied. "No, seriously. You've been kind of freaky lately. A few minutes ago, for instance. And then last night, when you had to go to the bathroom. You're not, like, breathing anthrax down there in the tomb, are you?"

Right in the middle of my forehead, between my eyebrows, a little ball of fire formed that would blossom into a headache if I didn't get some fluids. I'd been in the desert long enough to recognize the symptoms of dehydration. I downed a swig of root beer to give myself some time to think. The sharp taste helped revive me a little. "I'm fine," I said in a reassuring way. "Nothing's bugging me at all. I'm fine. See? Perfectly calm. I'm fine."

"I saw Jan slip it onto your tray." While I'd been talking, Connor had sat on the bench next to me and maneuvered his lips close to my ear.

"*What?*" I yelled. For someone who'd just professed to be fine and bug-free, I was doing a mighty good impression of a total wig-out.

"Be calm," murmured Connor, loading his shawarma onto flatbread. "Laugh. Smile. Pretend you're having fun."

"Ha-ha-ha-ha-ha!" I sounded like a freakin' maniac. Connor joined in. I surely hoped it looked like we were having some private joke together. Maybe it worked, because from across the mess tent, Jan sent me a look of sheer loathing. "I'm gonna kill her."

Sue gave me a look, rolled her eyes, and commented to Mallorie, "*Les* couples *dans l'amour sont* wacko."

"You knew it had to be her, didn't you?"

To be honest, there were a few moments when I'd once again thought the bracelet might be cursed. "Are you sure?" I said out the side of my mouth.

"I was outside looking in." He switched from his confidential voice to a normal lunch voice. "Good turnovers today, huh?"

"De-lish!" I lied. Deidre was right; mine already was covered with sand from the breeze. I went back to growling. "The thing is, I dropped it off on her tray and it took me only about forty seconds to get back to this side of the room. How could she get it, run over here, and hide it in forty seconds without me seeing?"

"I'm telling you, I saw her do it," Connor repeated. Sue and Bo and Mallorie gaped at us from the other side of the table. Oh, yes, the way we were talking to each other without moving our lips was quite the show, all right. All we needed was the ventriloquist's dummies and we'd be all set for high school amateur night.

"Fine, fine!" I didn't know how in the world January James might have pulled off that particular stunt, but I didn't care. She might be trying to set me up to be caught with the stolen bracelet—honestly, was she *that* jealous I'd kissed Seth twice?—but now she knew I was onto her. I started to rise to my feet, never letting my eyes leave that freckled face.

"Where are you going?" Connor stood up beside me.

"Is this the going-to-the-latrine show?" Bo asked Sue. "Because I caught it last night and don't need to see the matinee."

"I'm going to take my tray and bang it down over Jan's head," I announced. Honestly I hadn't intended to do any such thing, but when I spoke the words and played the image in my head like a movie clip, it started to sound better and better.

"Come with me," Connor said, grabbing my hand. I nearly fell backward over the bench as he yanked me in the direction of the door.

"Can I have your shawarma if you're done?" I heard Bo call out. "Hello?"

"I wasn't really going to do it!" I protested once we were outdoors. The sun was nearly directly overhead at that point. Instinctively Connor turned around his baseball cap to shield his eyes from the blaze. I had to make do with a hand held in a salute over my eyebrows. Nearby, an Egyptian man snored in the shade, his head wrapped against the glare. "I was kidding!"

"You need to cool down," he told me. Ironic, really, considering how he'd dragged me out into the sun during the hottest part of the day.

"I'm fine!"

"You keep saying that," he told me. "And you know what? I don't believe it." I started to smart-mouth him, but before I could say a word he added, "Said with affection."

That little ball of pain and stress started once more to burn in the center of my forehead. "I need my root beer," I said.

It took him only a moment to duck in and out of the mess tent to retrieve it for me. "Where's the bracelet?" he asked. I patted the pocket of my shirt. "I let you pull this crazy stunt against my better will," he said. "Do me a favor. Just head back to camp and rest awhile. Take your root beer with you. We'll figure this out later."

"There's nothing to figure out!" I practically shrieked. "You saw her put it under my napkin!"

"I'm talking about what we'll do *now*," he said. It was funny how his voice reassured me. The sound of it didn't completely erase my anger, but it soothed the rough edges. "Chloe." I felt compelled to look into his eyes. I saw safety there. "It'll be fine."

At last I nodded. "Okay," I said. "I don't really have a lot of experience with being a felon, that's all."

"You're not a felon," he said in a low, even voice. "You're just someone who's getting a pretty raw deal at the moment for some reason. That's all. Got it?"

"Yeah. Fine. I'll wait. Can I please hang out in your tent until the end of lunch?" The thought of meeting either Kathy or Dag in my own tent was unbearable. I'd rather lie down for a cuddly nap between the mummies of Tekhen and Tekhnet.

"You have to ask? You know you can." He looked at me with concern for a moment more. "Want me to bring your lunch when I come get you?"

"Nah. Let Bo have it." I grinned.

On the way back to his tent I was grateful for that small moment of sanity. Whenever I seemed to be walking on the tilting boards in some crazy funhouse, Connor had a way of giving me balance. He was the hand reaching out to guide me back to solid ground. Only this morning I'd had no clue of how that bracelet had ended up in my bed, and look—

we'd figured out that Jan James had been behind it. I was still a few steps away from decoding how she'd managed to get it off her tray and back onto my own so quickly, but I was way ahead of where I'd been only a few hours ago. Right?

Right, I assured myself. Everything would be okay. Connor and I would nail the solution sooner or later.

Sooner would be better.

I wasn't sure, once I entered the tent, whether I was in Connor and Bo's living quarters or Jekyll and Hyde's. One side was relatively neat, save for a pile of books at the foot of the cot that had gotten knocked over at some point. All the clothes were either folded into piles or neatly stored away in one of the duffels under the bed; even the cot's blanket had been pulled up and straightened. The other side . . . well. Ever since I learned the word in sixth grade vocabulary class I'd never really had the opportunity to use it: The other half was *squalid*. It made my brothers' rooms look tidy. I was used to the athletic sock/underwear/sweat/musky boy smell, but man! Who left their dirty shorts on their pillow?

Bo, apparently. I took the stupid bracelet from my pocket and plopped it down on Connor's little bedside table. I was sick of carrying it. Man, was I beat. For the umpteenth time since my arrival I envied kids around the world who were spending this month doing normal things, like going to school and doing their homework and hanging out in the mall. When I got back to Seattle, the rest of high school was going to seem like a year and a half of unadulterated vacation.

Stress does things to your body. It tenses up your shoulders and makes your back hurt. It creases your forehead and it clenches your butt. I hadn't realized what pain I really was in until I actually lay down on Connor's cot and rested my eyes for a minute. Connor's tent was *quiet.* Okay, it was a little bit on the smelly side on Bo's half, but man. A girl could do some serious sleeping here at this time of day. Weren't there, like, whole countries where they took siestas in the middle of the day after lunch? Wouldn't that be the absolute . . .

"Hey, sleepyhead." I pulled my eyes open reluctantly. How embarrassing! Napping was really the last thing I'd intended to do. Connor must have sensed my shame, because he smiled down at me and brushed some hair away from my eyes.

"Crud." I tried sitting up, but a little thing called gravity pulled me back down. I waited a minute for my head to stop spinning. "Am I late? How long was I out?"

"You couldn't have been out more than twenty or twenty-five minutes," Connor said. He perched on the edge of Bo's cot, opposite, while I struggled to sit up. "And you're just a little late. I wouldn't have let you sleep all afternoon, though. My dad says that twenty-five-minute naps are—"

"Voices? I am hearing the voices?" From outside the tent I heard a singsong accent, followed by the sound of footsteps.

Any of the relaxation I'd gained from my short rest suddenly vanished. "Double crud," I growled. "Rona McDonald."

"Hellooooo?" An enormous wedge of carrot-red hair suddenly intruded itself into the tent, followed by the rest of Dagmar. I could tell she was at her bossiest when she shook her finger at us. The gesture always made me feel guilty even when I hadn't done anything wrong. "I am feeling the surprise! When I am hearing voices outside, I am thinking it is Beauregard Merenees, Marnees. . . ."

"Mereness," Connor corrected.

"Yes, Marines, and instead who am I finding? Of all pipple, I am not expecting them to be you two, in here, alone together. Are you making the kiss-kiss? Yes? When you should be working?"

"No!" we both exclaimed. I mean, it was like the one time we *weren't* making the kiss-kiss that she'd decided we were up to something.

"Chloe was looking tired, so I told her to take a rest in here . . ." Connor began. While he was explaining, though, I suddenly remembered something. I'd put the stolen bracelet on Connor's bedside table, where it was still lying in full sight. Stupid, stupid, stupid Chloe!

Have you ever been in your room at home and had your mom come in the room when there's something sitting around you didn't want her to see? I'm not talking about anything illegal, or something like a shirtless boyfriend. I mean something simple, like your diary or a poem you'd just written or maybe instant messages from your buds all over your computer screen when you'd sworn up and down you were sweating over homework. Here's what happens. You tell yourself not to look at whatever it is. If you look at it, you'll just draw your mom's attention to it, and then you'll have her prying into your business just like she has none of her own to mind.

It was like that with Dag in the room. *Flick.* My eyes darted sideways to see if the bracelet was still on the table.

Don't do that! I thought. My eyes flicked back to Connor, still explaining.

Flick. Still there? Had it maybe sprouted wings and flown off?

Stop that! Eyes back front!

Flick.

What's wrong with you?!

Flick.

". . . so then I stopped back here and . . ." Connor had been watching my eyes jerk back and forth as if I were following an invisible tennis match. On the last flick he looked over at the little table. ". . . woke her up so we could . . ." He gaped, and stopped talking. ". . . get back to work," he finished weakly.

Too late, though. Dag had seen him turn his head. Her attention instantly leaped across the tent. What a long, sickening moment that was. Hot and sweaty flashes alternated with cold and sticky moments, one right after the other. Connor looked as if he were going to throw up. I already felt as if I were halfway there. I was going to be caught. I was going to be the first person thrown out of Dig Egypt! in years.

I wouldn't have been surprised right then if our chaperone had started yelling at us, or throwing around accusations, but I wasn't at all expecting what happened next: Dag hissed. She actually drew back, opened her mouth, and hissed like a cat! That reaction almost frightened me more than my impending doom. "That . . . that . . . !" She staggered in its direction with a finger outstretched, trembling. Then, "Where . . . where . . . !"

I jumped up. My feet raised a little cloud of dust on the ground when I landed. "Um. It's like this." Was I really going to have to admit my guilt? How could I? I was the good girl!

156

"It's mine!" Connor said, scrambling upright. That shut my mouth. Only for a moment, though.

"We didn't steal it, honest," I said, glaring at him. My voice sounded as if I'd taken a hit of helium from a rubber balloon. "It was in a mound of rubble in the burial chamber."

Connor was desperately trying to keep me from saying more. He waved his hands around and made faces at me. Dag gave him a sharp look, then looked back at me. "How is it getting there?" she snapped.

"I don't know! I just . . . !" The more I tried to summon the words to explain my innocence, the harder it was to force them out.

"I am seeing." Dag scowled. She rapped one of her nails on her front tooth so that it made a little *tick-tick-tick* sound. "I am seeing how it is. *You* are stealing precious artifact and dragging poor little girl to jail with you!" She swung around and pointed at Connor.

"No!" I yelled. How in the world could she be so dense?

"Yes," Connor said, at the same time.

"Don't you dare!" I wanted to slap him right at that moment.

"Look, Ms. Sorensson," Connor said, ignoring me. "I found it in the excavation. I told Chloe about it, and we didn't know what to do."

"Stop it!" I yelled. Just because I couldn't admit the truth was no reason for him to cover for me.

"We didn't steal it. That's the truth. Neither of us has even *been* in the artifact trailer."

Dagmar was back to tapping her tooth again. A weird thought occurred to me, though. If she was so certain that one of us had stolen the darned thing, why had she been so frightened of the bracelet a minute before? You don't get scared of a stolen object. Maybe she was worried she'd lose her job if one of her charges committed theft? I didn't quite get it. I had other things on my brain, though. Why was Connor being so stupid and self-sacrificing and *stupid* and . . . well, sweet?

How is it that a person you want to hug to bits can at the same time make you want to pop him one? Life is so screwed up.

"Egyptian jail is being no place for young boys," she said at last. I thought I saw Connor's face turn slightly white at that comment. I was pretty sure that as up close and personal as Connor wanted to get with the country, that was going a little far. "And I am liking the both of you. Sweet childrens, both. Sit, sit."

Connor and I gave each other a wide-eyed, eye-popping stare, but we obeyed. I didn't know which was more frightening: Dagmar the walking pain in the rear, or sugary Dagmar who wanted to be our friend. After removing several socks and dropping them to the floor using only her fingernails, the Swedish woman sat down on Bo's cot opposite us. She adjusted her Dig Egypt! T-shirt. "Such good childrens, so smart! Dagmar is thinking she will help you."

"How?" Connor asked. The mention of jail had frightened him badly, I think.

Dag smiled. "I will be taking bracelet and making rid of it for you. Is bad thing. Cursed! Brings you both much unhappiness!"

That was certainly the unvarnished truth right there. Connor screwed his face up, though. "I won't allow it if you're planning to destroy it or sell it. That bracelet's an important artifact."

Now it was Dag's moment to turn slightly pale. "I never

mean such thing!" she said. "How is childrens thinking this? No, no, no, no, no." She was emphatic here. "I will be taking foul, filthy bracelet and giving to Dr. Massad. I am being very good friends with Dr. Massad! He is not wishing for trouble either. But we must all be very, very quiet. No words! Not even to each other!"

Connor's jaw jutted out. It was his stubborn look. "I don't want Chloe's name mentioned at all," he insisted.

"Stop that!" I told him. He swung his head around and raised his eyebrows. I closed my mouth again. I didn't want Chloe's name mentioned, either.

Dag laughed lightly. "No names mentioned! None sowhatever! Chloe is being one of our best students here in all the years of the program!"

Hey, that didn't exactly jibe with what she'd said only a few days before. Connor must have been thinking the same thing, because he spoke up. "You've given her two warnings. I don't want her getting a third."

"Is the nuisance of my life that I am being cursed with the heart of a mother but my tenderloins give me no childrens of my own," Dag murmured in a tone so sickly that under any other circumstances it would have made me gag. She smiled at me with her crooked teeth. "We will pretend other two warnings did not happen, eh? Was being only the tough love."

"Is this because you're worried it might look bad on you?" I asked her. She gave me a sharp look, and I meekly added, "I mean, it might seem like you don't have control over us or something."

"Yes!" That had been almost too easy. She was back to sugary again. "Exactly that, and because Dagmar likes you childrens so much! Now, what are you thinking? Yes? Is best for everyone, yes? All problems solved?"

I looked at Connor. Connor looked at me. We tried to judge each other's reactions to this tricky proposition.

Rapidly as I could, I considered our options. We could refuse, and have the adult in charge of our welfare turn us in. Or we could agree, and go along with it, and get off scot-free. Dag had offered us a mandate, and I didn't see any other way out.

I shrugged slightly. *Say something,* I thought, hoping Connor had another option.

He shook his head. "I guess," he said, very slowly, "I guess we don't have a choice."

Dagmar beamed. "Oh, I knew you childrens would agree. Is best for all." She stood up from the cot and plucked the bracelet from the table. A strange look appeared in her eyes when she held it. I supposed she was not happy about having to touch anything she thought was cursed. "Now run along, run along back to your little works," she urged, shooing the pair of us from the tent. "And remember—do not let the lips spill words to no one!"

Outside in the sun, the entire few preceding minutes seemed almost unreal. The encounter with Dag had been like a bad nightmare, a fairy-tale trip to the gingerbread house in the middle of the forest, a dream that disappeared in the glare and intensity of the Egyptian heat. I could tell by Connor's watch that we were close to a half hour late to our afternoon assignments.

Neither of us spoke a word during most of the trip back to the valley. Finally, though, I couldn't hold it in any longer. "You shouldn't have said it was your fault. I understand why you did, but . . . thank you."

"I think we made the right choice." Connor waited until we were at the bottom of the sloping path to finish that thought. "But it's out of our hands, right? That's the important thing."

"Yeah, that's the important thing."

At least I hoped it was.

What a weird day I had. I'd spent the morning racked with paranoia. The afternoon I should have spent feeling relieved—but I couldn't. What was wrong with me?

Have you ever been to a play or a musical at the theater, and you get to the end of the first big act, when the hero and the heroine are, you know, holding hands during the French Revolution or reunited under the opera house or have just had their first kiss? It's great. It should be satisfying. At the same time, though, you go out for intermission knowing there's a whole other act to go, and besides, you saw the villain twiddling his mustache in the background. Something big is going to go down between acts.

That was what this reprieve felt like. Intermission. I just couldn't shake the feeling that we'd screwed up, somehow, and that the curtain would soon lift and we'd find everything ruined. And after we separated, I couldn't ask Connor if he felt the same way.

Late in the afternoon, shortly before dinner, I found myself alone with Eddie Loret for a few minutes up at camp. We were cleaning the instruments we'd been using for the day, wiping the trowel blades clean and setting them into the locked cabinet where they would spend the night. By then, my warning instinct was blinking so rapidly from thinking the situation through so many times that I couldn't help myself. "Do you trust Dagmar?" I blurted, without even so much as an explanation.

He blinked. "She's worked with Dig Egypt! for years," he said. "Why wouldn't I?" Eddie's usually pleasant expression darkened slightly. "Is this about the water issue again?"

"Never mind," I said. "Shouldn't have asked."

"Chloe, I know you kids are used to more frequent baths and cleaner clothes, but out here in the desert . . ."

I should have known better than to mention my doubts to an adult. They all stick together in the end. "Just pretend I never opened my mouth, Eddie. Okay?"

Eddie would probably forget it the minute we separated. I only wished I could. I was waiting for intermission to end.

Eleven

No music signaled an end to my brief interlude from worry. The concession stands didn't close; nor did I hear rustling from backstage. The lights didn't blink to give me a warning. The curtains simply rose with six words: "Connor Marsh. Please come with me."

We had just reached the top of the hill on our way to lunch the next day. I was starving; for breakfast I hadn't eaten anything more than a stale toasted bagel, and I'd been looking forward to something more substantial. It was just like any other late morning. Bo was making fun of Deidre. Mallorie and Sue were babbling at each other in incomprehensible *Franglais*. Connor and I were walking at the front of our little desert family, holding hands and letting the occasional squeeze do our talking for us. It felt familiar; after two and a half weeks, the lunchtime ritual felt like a bit of home away from home.

Eddie Loret stood waiting for us, his hands planted on his hips. I didn't notice the coldness in his eyes until we tried to walk past him. I'd assumed he wanted to take the path down, himself, but instead his arm shot out and grabbed Connor's shoulder. Then he uttered those six words.

Not to be dramatic or anything, but I wanted to sink down to my knees and beg for mercy. I think I knew better than Connor what was coming. "What's the matter, Eddie?" Sue asked.

The archaeologist didn't answer her. "Come on, buddy," he told Connor. "Game's up."

I didn't want to let go of Connor's hand. "What game?" I babbled, though I knew the answer. Kathy Klemper emerged from her tent then, her arms crossed. She watched the action from a few paces away.

"Chloe," Eddie said, level and calm, "this is between Connor, Dr. B., and me."

Connor gave my hand a final clutch. "No!" I cried. I could guess what had happened. Eddie had become suspicious by my question the night before, gone to Dagmar, and she had crumbled and told him that Connor had taken the bracelet. Maybe she'd gone to Eddie herself and ratted on him. Or maybe she'd gone to Dr. Massad and he hadn't believed a word of it. Damn Dagmar Sorensson! Everything was all her fault! I *knew, knew, knew* I shouldn't have allowed her to pretend to be our friend.

I'd expected to see panic in Connor's eyes, but instead I only saw calmness and resignation. How in the world had he known this was coming? Had he distrusted Dag, too? "Whatever happens," he said in a low voice, "know that things are going to be okay."

"Connor . . ."

"Don't worry," he whispered. He put a hand to the side of my face, butted his forehead gently against mine, and gazed deep into my eyes. "Don't be scared."

Then he was gone. A cloud of dust billowed into the air while he and Eddie walked away at top pace. "What was that about?" Sue demanded.

"It's all my fault." I wanted to cry. Everything seemed so black at that moment. My mom's fond of saying that it's always darkest before the dawn, but I didn't believe it. There wasn't going to be any dawn. Not here, not now. "It's my fault."

"What's your fault?" When I didn't answer, Sue came over and shook me lightly. "Chloe! What's going on?"

They all wanted answers from me, the brave one. They wanted reassurances that I couldn't possibly give. I wanted to blurt to them all that I wasn't what they thought I was—but when I opened my mouth to let the doubts come out, the first thing I noticed was how frightened their faces were. They knew something serious had just happened and were upset. Why add my own burdens to theirs?

I swallowed, took a deep breath, and tried to sound calm. "I think it's nothing," I told them. "I think I might have gotten Connor into some trouble with Dag. That's all."

Bo murmured to Deidre, "I told you there was something up with them."

Attempting to keep my voice light, I cocked my head and smiled. "You guys go ahead to lunch," I told them. "I'll just follow and see what's up. Okay?" No one moved. "Go on," I repeated. "I swear, I'll come in just a few minutes."

I waited for them to head off before I dared move. I didn't want to see me run. As I turned to follow Eddie and Connor's route, Kathy stepped forward from the spot where she'd been watching. "*I* know what's happening," she told me. "That boyfriend of yours is being sent packing."

"How do you know?" I demanded, angry at her and the world.

"I hear things," she taunted. "You'd better hurry if you expect to say good-bye."

My pride warred with my instincts. I wanted to run as fast as my legs could carry me, but at the same time I didn't want Kathy to get any satisfaction from my exit. I settled on a fast walk out of camp that turned into a desperate sprint as soon as her sour little face was out of sight.

Don't be scared, Connor had told me. How could I not be scared? I thought of all the fearful moments I'd endured lately, starting with the month of stomachaches beforehand, the needles I'd endured for my inoculations, the terror I'd felt with every jolt on the airplane ride, the noise and strangeness of Cairo. I'd tolerated dark tombs and injuries and people who couldn't speak my language. There had been ladders and scorpions and mummies whose faces in death I'd never be able to erase from my mind. I'd feared warnings and strangers and weird foods, and I'd worried about a bunch of stuff that never materialized: sandstorms, being lost in the desert, and, most of all, being the least popular kid here.

It was the last fear that drove me the entire time I'd been in Egypt. I'd transformed myself into the biggest, the bravest, and the most outspoken, just so that no one would ever guess what I was really like inside. I'd used up so much energy fretting that I hadn't thought about anyone but myself.

In a way it's funny that all those other worries—even the worst of them, like the deadly scorpions and the unearthly faces of the twin manicurists, dead and forgotten for so many years—were nothing compared to my anxiety at that moment. What I felt wasn't fear for myself or what might happen to me, but for someone else. Even when Seth had hurt himself, I hadn't been this miserable.

When I reached the clearing where Eddie and Dr. Battista's trailer sat, I could already hear Eddie's stern voice inside. Strain though I tried, I couldn't pick out his words. I ran dirty fingers through my hair and sat down on a plastic lawn chair sitting just outside the door. This was awful. I rocked myself back and forth, sweaty and tense. I knew what I had to do, but doubted I could carry it through. I had to. I simply had to.

I didn't want to be sent home in disgrace. The thought of my parents' disappointment scared me worse than any scorpion on earth, even one with a radioactive stinger from a bad science fiction movie. Forever after I'd be known as a thief and a liar.

I thought of Connor looking out on the desert landscape, though, and how he drank it in with his eyes as if it were the precious water we all craved, and how not even the deepest gulps completely slaked his thirst. My heart ached for him. I knew I couldn't let him suffer.

What did it mean when you cared more about someone else's happiness and safety than for your own? Was that love?

Love was supposed to feel good. Whatever this feeling was that squirmed inside me, it hurt.

I looked up at the sky, my eyes dazed by its impossible blueness. I resolved right then and there that Connor would remain to see another of those Egyptian skies, and another after that. He'd spend his term here. I'd be the one going home.

I stood up from the chair, dusted myself off, and yanked open the trailer door. "Leave Connor alone!" I announced, drawing back my shoulders to appear dignified. My heart beat so quickly I was certain they'd be able to see it thudding beneath the fabric of my shirt.

As I expected, Dr. Battista and Eddie stood on either side of a seated Connor. Both of the archaeologists had their arms crossed. They looked up in astonishment at my loud and sudden entrance. I cleared my throat and spoke again. "He's done nothing wrong. It was my fault."

Connor had been sitting hunched over, his elbows resting on his knees while he ran his fingers through his curls. My triumphant announcement was intended to uplift his spirits, but if anything he just looked . . . strange. Dr. Battista cleared her throat. "Chloe, this really isn't the time."

"Let him go," I demanded. "Take me instead. I'm the troublemaker here."

At that statement Connor broke into a broad grin, unfolded his limbs, rose to his feet, and started walking through the mess of papers and maps over to me. "I knew you'd do something like this," he said, laughing. Laughing? I didn't get it.

"I'm the one who—"

His hand closed over my mouth. "Chloe," Connor said meaningfully. "Shut up."

"Hold on, hold on," Eddie said. "I'm interested to hear. Chloe, did you know about this all along?"

I tried to shake my head with vigor, but Connor was already talking. "Chloe didn't know anything about me running away from home."

What?

He let go of me then. I gaped at him a moment. "You ran . . . huh?"

"I ran away from home to come here," he explained. "That's the big funky secret I kept from you. I didn't want you involved, remember?" I nodded slowly. I'd known that something had been bothering him for a long time.

Connor paced back to his chair and sat down again. "You guys don't understand how much I *wanted* to be here," he said to the archaeologists. "I applied and got the scholarship and my whole life was great. I was finally going to be doing the one thing I wanted more than anything else. But right before . . . well, about two weeks before I was about to go, my mom started to worry. She didn't want me missing school. She didn't like the thought of me being halfway across the world. It was, like, all she talked about. I'd wake up in the mornings and she'd already be going on and on about how I could be killed by asps or crazy Egyptians. She didn't like me being anywhere near the Middle East in case of terrorism or hijackings. She got so hysterical. It was crazy."

I listened to the confession, amazed. I saw Dr. Battista shooting glances in my direction from time to time, but my surprise was absolutely 100 percent genuine. I hadn't known a single thing. "Finally all the fretting got to my dad," Connor continued. "He said that if he had to listen to one more word of my mom's nonsense he'd either be locked up in an asylum for the insane, or in jail for murder. It was a toss-up which. He was kidding," he added hastily, looking at us to be sure we knew it was a joke. Eddie nodded at him to keep going. "So that was it. They shredded my plane ticket and called the university to tell them I wouldn't be going. But I *had* to come!"

"So you lied to your folks?" Eddie asked.

Connor shook his head. "See, I still had my passport from when we lived in Australia a couple of years ago, and I'd already gone through all my inoculations, and the ticket was paid for by the university . . . so it seemed a shame. . . ." He swallowed and put back on his cap. "I called the university back and pretended to be my dad. I told them my son Connor would still be going to Egypt after all, but he'd arrive a couple of days late. Then I went online and exchanged my ticket for one a couple of days later. I don't think my folks have ever heard of an electronic ticket." He grinned, for my benefit. "And then I pretended to be really down about not coming here on the day I was supposed to leave, and again the day after. On the third day I left a note saying I was so upset I was hitchhiking to Vermont. My older brother lives there with his girlfriend."

"And you came here instead." Connor looked at me and nodded in agreement to my words. "Because you had to be here. Dr. Battista, you can't send him away," I said suddenly. "There's only a week left. Don't you remember what you told me? About people living in fear who don't hear the call? And about those of us who do?"

"Chloe," she said gently.

"Look at everything he did to get here! It's not fair!"

"It's not fair," she agreed. "But Connor's mother has been very upset."

"She's been a pain in the ass," Eddie said. "She called the American consulate here once she finally figured out you weren't dead along some highway between Seattle and Vermont, and once her plane landed she had Dr. Tousson out of bed at four in the morning. I understand your drive to be here and I can't say I don't respect it, but what you did to your mother was cruel," he added.

"She's here?" I asked.

Connor looked at me and nodded slowly. "In Cairo. She'll be here tonight to get me. We'll be flying home tomorrow."

"You can't," I said, shaking my head. I didn't want to admit it could be happening.

"I knew Mom and Dad would figure it out sooner or later," Connor said. "It was always a matter of time. I just hoped it would be, you know, later, is all." I realized how true that was. He'd always spent every day here as if it were his last. He'd wanted to be in Egypt so badly that he'd plotted and planned and lived with the guilt of deceiving his parents, while I'd just resented mine for locking me in my desert prison. I'd spent every day wishing it were my last. Why hadn't I been truly brave, like Connor?

What a lot of my life I'd wasted, fearing everything. It all seemed so stupid now. So much time squandered.

Dr. Battista took a step in the direction of the satellite phone, retrieved a slip of paper, and punched out a number. "I'd like you to talk to her," she said to Connor in a soft tone. "Reassure her you're all right. We'll leave you alone."

Connor regarded the phone with horror. "I . . . I can't," he whispered.

When I reached out with my hand to turn his head so I could look into his eyes, I saw fear there. It was as familiar as a map of my own neighborhood. If anyone could lead him through that fear, it was me. Chloe. Queen of Denial.

I crossed the trailer and took the receiver from Dr. Battista, nodding to let her know I'd help him make the call. "It'll be okay," I assured them.

I waited until the archaeologists had exited and clicked shut the door before I punched the button to send the number. On the other end I heard ringing. I pressed the phone into Connor's hand and helped him raise it to his ear. "Don't be scared," I whispered. "I'll be here."

His eyes flashed wide at the sound of someone on the other end. "Hello?" he said, his voice wobbly. "Mom?"

"Mon Dieu!" Sue ran over to us at top speed when we finally sauntered back into camp.

The group of them bounced over like they had gotten a sponsorship from the Pogo Stick Association of Egypt. Bo was hooting at the top of his lungs, Deidre wore the biggest grin I'd ever seen on her face, and Mallorie was singing a song that sounded vaguely familiar to me: *"Allons, enfants de la patrie!"*

"Oh my God oh my God oh my God!" Sue said, grabbing both of us and hopping like the Energizer bunny on fast-forward. "Where *were* you two? You've missed the best lunch *ever!*"

"Le jour de la gloire est arrivé!" sang Mallorie, her clenched fist raised high in the air.

The heck! "Guys, what is going on?" I wanted to know.

Connor, still recuperating from his phone call, managed a smile. "Did we get the day off or something? More water?"

"Yes, yes, yes, and *so* much more, my fine friend," Bo said, strutting around in a way that reminded me of a game-show host.

"They've arrested Dag!" Deidre shouted. "At lunch! You missed it!"

"What?" Connor and I both shouted.

"Just come see for yourself!" Sue crowed, and they all ran ahead of us back to the clearing in front of the mess tent. I looked at Connor; he looked at me. We both grinned broadly and ran after them.

Her orange hair crumpled and askew, Dag was being dragged out from the mess tent into an all-terrain vehicle by two Egyptian men in uniform who carried wicked-looking guns. Watching from the sidelines along with all the rest of the camp, students and scientists alike, were Eddie and Dr. Battista. Eddie leaned over to whisper something to his boss. Instantly I felt a pang of guilt. What had I done? "I didn't mean to get her thrown in *jail!*" I yelled, appalled with myself.

"You?" I felt, rather than heard, someone step to my side. It was Seth, his sun-kissed muscles glistening. He was holding hands with a freckled redhead—January James. I was so utterly amazed at the sight of Dag in handcuffs that I completely forgot any bad feelings I had toward Jan. "What did you do?" Seth asked.

"I . . . I told Eddie and Dr. Battista that Dag was a water thief!" I said. "They're going to put her in jail for *that?*"

Everyone started talking at once. "Not water theft. Theft theft," I picked out Bo saying.

"I guess she'd been stealing artifacts from the various digs around here for years," Seth told me over the chatter, never letting go of Jan's hand. I wanted to think her expression was smug, but every time she looked up at him, whatever was in her eyes was genuine enough that it made me want to look away out of politeness. Of course, it made me want to grab Connor's hand, too. Jan wasn't the only person who had gotten herself a hottie this trip. "She'd been using her position to rifle through the dig sites at night; then she and her brothers would sell the artifacts in Cairo. I'm guessing she was probably even in the tomb the night that you and I were exploring the shaft."

Jan looked furious right then, and even I felt compelled to add over my shoulder to Connor, "That's not nearly as bad as it sounds. You know, I thought I heard someone in there with us!"

"That ladder accident might not have been as accidental as I thought." Seth nodded.

Jan kissed her fingers and applied them to Seth's forehead. "Poor baby," she said. Right as I was thinking that someone should, like, totally kill me if I ever did anything so possessive to Connor, Jan said directly to me, "The Department of Antiquities guys caught Dagmar with stolen bracelets. Stolen . . . *twin* . . . bracelets."

Oh, my. Suddenly everything started to make sense.

Twin bracelets. I'd even seen indistinguishable bracelets

in the antechamber's frescos, hanging from the wrists of Tekhen and Tekhnet as they shared a meal together. Identical twin bracelets. For identical twins.

Jan seemed as smug as a slug in a jug as she laid it out for us. "She'd already sold one of the bracelets. I bought mine in a shop in Cairo. But the one you dug up threw her for a loop when she found you had it. The DOA caught her with both—yours in her tent after she took it from you guys, mine in her pocket. After that, let's just say it didn't take her long to confess to everything. When a bracelet she thought she'd stole showed up here at the dig, she really did begin to think it was cursed."

"Oh, sheeeee!" I made a huge show of rolling my eyes. "What kind of idjut believes in curses?" I thought about everything for a minute while they laughed at my impression of Dag. But I'd planted my bracelet in Dagmar's backpack that first night! How could . . . I looked at Jan's bag, sitting on the ground. Oh man! It had a blue patch like Dag's! Then I hadn't put it in Dagmar's pack at all! And it wasn't my bracelet I found under my pillow a few minutes later! It had been the copy that Jan had somehow found and slipped to me. And the next night, when I'd put that bracelet on Jan's tray . . . she'd returned mine to me! We'd been swapping bracelets back and forth the entire time, like total spazzes. "So you *don't* have a magic watch that stops time!" I yelled.

Everyone halted whatever they were doing to stare in my direction. "Excuse me?" Jan asked at last, narrowing her eyes like I was the biggest idiot on earth.

"Never mind." My lips were dry from all the excitement. I pulled out my lip gloss and applied a protective layer. "I feel so stupid! I thought my bracelet was cursed, but it's more like some dumb episode of *I Love Lucy,* only I'm Lucy and you're Ethel," I told Jan.

"Yes, except *I'm* Lucy," Jan argued good-naturedly. "You know, Chloe, you were really mean, hiding that bracelet in my stuff."

"You did it to me!" I pointed out.

"Whatever. I got what I wanted in the end. Right?" she asked Seth. He answered her with a peck on the lips.

"Two bracelets!" I crowed to Connor. "Two!"

"Yeah." He grinned at me, and then leaned forward for a peck of his own. "I heard that part." He grabbed my hand. "Two bracelets. Did you get what you wanted in the end, too?" he said to me, his voice barely audible over the babble of the assembly.

"Yes," I told him. "Oh, yes." My heart was glad to say it.

Yet it was the first occasion I had had to look at Connor and know that our remaining time together could be measured in hours.

Twelve

The first time I really talked to Connor, it had been a starry evening with a full moon. Though the stars shone just as brightly the night he left, the moon had withered away. It hung above us in the sky like an illustration from *Arabian Nights,* its edges sharp as any knife. Soon it would wane away to nothing, and the Muslims would celebrate the three-day feast that signaled the end of their holy month of Ramadan. The music we heard now came from Sue's tent, where Mallorie was teaching the other kids—even Kathy Klemper—dirty songs in French.

I heard him sigh beside me. "Okay. I've got to go. Promise you won't cry."

"I can't promise that, dope," I told him. "But I promise to hold it in until after you leave."

"I hate the thought of you crying." His voice was gentle as he took my hands in his and gave me the last kiss we would share over the valleys of the Egyptian desert.

"Get over it quick," I warned him. "It'll happen again. I'm a very emotional girl."

"I'll find that out for myself. I mean, we're only going to be separated a week, right?"

"Right," I said. In only a little over a week we'd both be back at North Seattle High together. A pang of doubt made me hesitate. "You will still be my friend back home, right? This won't be like *Grease,* where I'm Olivia Newton-John and I get to school after we've had our summer lovin' and you're all standoffish and Travolta-y on me?"

"I won't be Travolta-y on you," he said. In the darkness, I could sense his smile. "We'll still be more than friends."

"Good."

Hand in hand, we walked away from the vista, past the camp and its singing voices, past the archaeologists' tents with their sounds of radios and snoring, enjoying the quiet. Finally we reached the clearing where a car waited, motor purring. I heard one of its windows roll down. "I guess I'll never see the Ramesseum," Connor said suddenly. "Will you take some photos?"

"Hey," I told him. He had to hear it from me—I couldn't let this go unsaid. "I'm really going to *live* this week. I'm going to keep my eyes open. I'm going to notice the colors and the scents and the way things sound, and when I get back home you'll hear all about it. It'll be almost like you were there. I promise."

Had I said the right words? From the expression on his face, as virtuous and kind as those of any of the smiling ancient Egyptian figures we had seen on frescoed walls, it seemed I had. "I'll hold you to that promise." His voice was choked and cracked with emotion. We both laughed a little, feeling the crunch of gravel underfoot as we shuffled uncomfortably. "Okay. Until next week, then?"

"Until next week."

I watched as he slid into the car, where his mother had been nice enough to wait while we took our last walk to the cliff's edge. His bags were already in the trunk; in a few short hours he would be back in the Cairo airport boarding a plane for Paris, and then for home.

When was it I could start crying? I began bargaining with myself to hold my tears until I'd seen the last of the car's taillights, when his head appeared out the window. "Hey," he called. "My mom said I should ask if there's anything you want us to tell your parents. I could call them back in Seattle."

"Tell them . . ." I hesitated. What should I say?

The answer came pretty simply. "Tell them I'm having the time of my life," I instructed, grateful to have the chance to pass on the message. "And tell them that when I come home, they won't believe how much I've changed."

Deep down inside, I knew nothing could be truer.

Historical Note

The fictional Valley of the Servitors is based on Egypt's Tombs of the Nobles, a large complex of ancient burial chambers and mastabas on the western bank of modern-day Luxor. Although archaeologists and historians believe thousands of tombs lie hidden in this area, only eight hundred or so of them have been excavated and studied.

Among the many tombs of ancient Egypt is the mastaba of Niankhkhnum and Khnumhotep, brothers, and perhaps twins, who in life were the honored manicurists of King Niuserre of the Fifth Dynasty. As the king's manicurists, the brothers were highly venerated and respected and held priestly duties in Egypt's complex state religion; they were even regarded as prophets of the sun god Ra.

Think about that the next time you have your nails done!

Don't miss Jan's side of the story in

EYELINER
OF THE
GODS

by Katie Maxwell

Turn the page for a sneak preview. . . .

ANCIENT MUMMY CURSE ENDED
BY INTREPID TEEN!

CAIRO *(JanNews)*: Sixteen-year-old American January James arrived in Egypt earlier this month and single-handedly solved a centuries-old curse attached to the mummy of . . .

"Crap. What was the name of the person who lived in the tomb?"

The woman sitting next to me on the bus pursed her lips and squinted her eyes at my notebook.

"Sorry," I said, sliding my hand over it so she couldn't read what I'd written. "This is confidential. I'm a journalist. Or I will be someday. I'm hoping to sell a couple of my stories about my time at the dig, so I'm sure you understand if I can't show it to you now. Do you get the *Shocking News Today!* here in Egypt?"

The woman, who wore a white head scarf called a hijab, flared her nostrils at me and looked away as if she'd smelled something bad. I did a covert pit-sniff check just in case my deodorant had given way on me after the long flight from Paris—the heat in Cairo was enough to strip the air from your lungs—but the Ps checked out okay, so

I just figured that she must be one of the conservative women Mrs. Andrews had told me about in her "dos and don'ts of going to Egypt" lecture. Most of the stuff she had told me was about how to be polite in another country, but some of it concerned how women were treated.

"I'm not wicked or anything because I'm traveling alone," I explained to the woman. She didn't look very convinced. In fact, she tried to avoid my eyes, but I felt it was important that the first person I talked to in Egypt *not* have the wrong impression of me. Start off as you mean to proceed, my mom always says. "Mrs. Andrews—she's our school principal—told me that Islamic rules say that men aren't supposed to harass women they don't know, but some men don't pay attention to the rules and look for women traveling on their own, figuring they're slut city, but I'm not. Just in case you were wondering. I don't even have a boyfriend! My sister April tried to give me Stan, her old boyfriend, but I draw the line at hand-me-down boyfriends."

The woman's nose looked pinched, as if she were trying not to breathe while sitting next to me. She glanced around the bus, obviously looking for another seat, but it was standing room only in the airport-to-Cairo bus.

"There was this guy last year whom I really liked, a senior, and man, I'm telling you, he was all that and a bag of chips, but he didn't even know I was alive, and I heard later from my friend Mina that he went off to be a monk or something, so that's probably why he didn't notice what guys usually notice about me."

I peered down at my chest. Even wearing April's loose Big Apple tee, my boobs were right there where anyone could stare at them. And guys did. The dawgs. Like I could help having big breastages?

"Anyway, Mrs. Andrews said that in Egypt I shouldn't make eye contact with unknown men, or be nice to them, or anything like that, but that it was okay to be nice to a woman, which is why I'm talking to you. Only"—I bit my lip and tucked my pencil into the spiral top of the notebook—"what if the woman I talk to is lesbian? Would that be the same thing as talking to a man? What if she's a weirdo, into all sorts of pervy things like bondage and stuff? Wouldn't that be just as bad as being nice to a regular guy? And what about gay guys? Are they okay to talk to? Man, this being-polite-to-people-in-a-different-culture stuff is hard when they don't give you all the rules."

The woman, her eyes now tinged with desperation, tried to slide away from me, but the bus was an old one, and there wasn't a lot of seat space, so she really didn't have anywhere to go as the bus crawled its way through downtown Cairo.

I looked at the woman a little more closely. "My name is Jan. It's short for January. And yes, before you ask, I was born in January. My dad named me. He named the last five of us, because Mom had run out of names by then. He died right after October was born, but it's okay, because I was only two, so I don't remember him or anything, and then Mom remarried Rob, who is really nice and can't have kids because he only has one noogie, so he got all ten of us with Mom. Rob's an artist, of course. Who else would marry my family?"

The bus swerved to the side, throwing the woman next to me up against my shoulder. She made a horrified gasping noise, and quickly dragged herself off of me, half rising out of the seat as she scanned the bus for somewhere else to sit.

I looked around, too, suddenly realizing that I had been so busy writing what was sure to be a killer story, not to mention reassuring my seatmate that I wasn't Jan the Wonder Ho, that I hadn't been watching for the stop the airport map showed was right next to my hotel. The bus, which earlier had been traveling down the busy downtown Cairo streets of offices and modern buildings, was now honking and swerving its way down a different part of town, where the streets were narrow, dark, and filled with as many people as cars. The old, scrungy buildings that lined the street were a solid mass of open-fronted stores overflowing with everything from leather bags to big brass things (water pipes?), wooden walking sticks, brightly patterned clothing and colorful scarves, jewelry, food, wicker baskets filled with who knew what, and a gazillion other things that I didn't have time to take in.

"Flash! You're lost, Jan," I said to myself as the bus slammed to a stop while a donkey was dragged across the street by a guy in a long white-and-black robe. Donkeys! Uh-oh—I'd gone from industrial, modern Cairo to something out of an old mummy movie in just the amount of time it took to tell a woman I wasn't a perv. "I'd better get out before I end up at the pyramids or who knows where," I muttered as I stuffed my notebook away in the bag that had been wedged between my feet. I hoisted all five hundred pounds of it, dragging both it and me into the aisle of the bus, groaning to myself about my luck in being so wrapped up in taking notes at the airport that I'd missed meeting the volunteer coordinator.

Worst-case scenario was that I'd have to walk. It couldn't be that far back to the touristy part of Cairo—I'd been gabbing for only a few minutes, after all. "And besides," I told the hijab woman's back as I followed her while she pushed her way out the door of the crowded bus, "I swore to myself before I left home that I was going to use this month in Egypt to lose all the blubber that my mother insists on calling puppy fat despite the fact that I'm not a puppy, and if I were, it would mean she was a b— Uh . . . never mind, I probably shouldn't say that word here. Mrs. Andrews said profanity was a big no-no. Hello? Mrs. Hijab Lady? *Bititkalimi ingleezi?* Poop!"

She didn't answer my question about whether or not she spoke English, but the way she melted into the crowd more or less answered the question. I slung my duffel bag strap over my shoulder and jumped out of the way when the bus started forward, coughing as the diesel fumes swallowed me in a blue-gray cloud of haze. I had to admit to being a bit worried about the fact that I was lost in a strange city.

"Come on, Jan, get a grip," I told myself as I started down the crowded sidewalk. "You want to be a journalist, and everyone knows that journalists always do exciting things like get lost in the middle of Cairo."

Someone grabbed my bare arm.

"Hey!" I whirled around and came face-to-face with a leering guy with ugly black and yellow teeth. He said something that I was sure wasn't nice at all. I shook my finger at him. "My principal told me about you! She also told me what to say: *Áram!* Evil!"

The guy blinked at me in surprise as I yelled the word at him, but I didn't wait to see how he was going to respond. I spun around and started walking quickly the way the bus had come, weaving my way through the crowds and stacks of things for sale, dodging dogs and donkeys and small boys sitting with wicker baskets of food who yelled at me as I went by. The noise was incredible—people were chatting, laughing, yelling, singing, and calling to each other over the dull throb of traffic, the blare of car horns an underscore to the loud, high-pitched singing from someone's radio, all of which blended with a thousand other noises that you don't know exist until you suddenly find yourself stranded half a world away from your home.

My stomach growled as I marched down the street, the spicy odor of cooking meat wafting out from one of the shops. The smell of the diesel belching out of the cars that worked their way down the street was nasty, but there were other scents that were a lot more pleasant—musk and patchouli from an incense place, the familiar smell of oranges from a nearby orange vendor, and lots of nummy restaurant smells that had me swallowing back gallons of saliva and reminding myself that I was supposed to be on a diet.

"It's not fair," I muttered as I stopped in front of a store that had the most delicious-looking pastries displayed on a cart. "Here I am in exotic Egypt, and I'm not allowed to eat anything but water and ice cubes."

Two people nearby stopped to stare at me. Belatedly I remembered that Mrs. Andrews had said I should always have a companion when touring the cities, but I hadn't intended on having to walk through half of Cairo to get to the hotel. I moved on.

"It's like this," I said to no one in particular, practicing the excuse I'd offer the volunteer coordinator as I lugged my bag (evidently now filled with lead and anvils and other hard, heavy things that were slowly dragging my shoulder down) through the quickly darkening narrow street. " 'I got lost at the airport and missed the group connection to the hotel.' "

Oh, yeah, that sounded lame. Lame-o-lame. Lamer than George W. Bush in jogging shorts.

"Um . . . maybe this is better. 'Sorry I missed you at the airport, Ms. Sorensson, but I had to go to the bathroom really badly. . . .' Ugh. No. She'll think I've got the big D if I say that. And I'd die if anyone thought I had the trots."

I came to a corner and paused. The street ahead narrowed even further, so no cars were able to drive down it, which, considering what I'd seen of Cairo drivers so far, was a blessing, but I was trying to retrace the bus's path.

"Okay, here's the deal—'I'm a journalist, and I was positive the guy in front of me at customs was a smuggler, so I had to hang around and take notes on him, and that's how I missed the meeting with you. . . .' " I sighed. "You know you're in trouble when the truth sounds weirder than fiction. You also know you're in trouble when you stand around talking out loud to yourself, especially when you have an audience."

My audience was apparently *not* appreciative of the fact that I had arrived in their city. A group of four guys in really ugly shirts lounging around outside what looked like a tobacco shop yelled catcalls across the street at me. The people walking around me gave me really unpleasant looks; even the women scowled as they tromped around me. Lost, alone, and without a good excuse for missing my contact at the airport, I turned to the left and tried to look innocent and not at all like a she-cat on the prowl for some lusty, busty action, praying all the while that I was heading in the direction of the Luxor Hotel.

"Moomkin almiss bizazeek?" The sneering voice, ac-

companied by a tug on my bag, had me spinning around, clutching the duffel bag tightly in case some of the street kids were thinking of doing a five-fingered rocket job on me. It wasn't the kids, though . . . it was the guys from the cigarette shop.

They were all pretty young, all but one in thin cotton shirts that looked like they were made out of the same material as my grandmother's kitchen curtains, and tight black pants. The guys weren't even cute, and if I have one rule in life, it's that the very least a guy who is going to hit on me can do is to be droolworthy. These guys weren't even remotely cute. They did, however, smell like they'd taken a bath in cheap men's cologne.

One of them, the one closest, teased his fingers through the wispy little bits of a beard that clung to his chin like snot on a doorknob. He said something else to me. I stuck my nose in the air, remembered I wasn't supposed to make eye contact with men (sheesh! So many rules just to come to one country!) and tried walking away, but Mr. Wimpy Beard had my bag.

"*Áram!*" I yelled at him, trying desperately to remember the other phrases the Dig Egypt! people had listed in their program guide as useful Arabic. There was something about saying "stop touching me" that was supposed to be useful . . . oh, yeah. "*Sibnee le wadi!*" I yelled at the top of my lungs.

I guess they weren't expecting me to yell, because two of the four hissed at me and backed off, but the other two, including Beard Boy, just laughed and tried tugging my bag toward them.

"Illegitimate sons of a donkey," I snarled, which was Rob's suggestion of a good insult. They didn't seem to get that at all, and Mr. Laughy Pants just laughed even harder, jerking me and my bag forward until he had a hand on my wrist.

I looked around for a woman to help me, like both Mrs. Andrews—who had been to Egypt before with the school choir—and the Dig Egypt! people had recommended, but the women who were scurrying by all had bags of groceries, and no one seemed to be inclined to help me.

"Okay, I can do this," I told myself, trying to pull free from the Bearded Wonder. "*Áram, áram!* This is going to make—*áram* already!—for a really great story. No newspaper will be able to resist buying it. I will probably win the Pulitzaaaaiiiii! *Take your hands off my arm!*"

While I was struggling with the first guy, the second one slipped behind me and copped a back-of-the-arm grope. Which just wigged me out. And he pinched, too. Hard! I jerked my hand and bag away from the Beard Weenie, stomped on the foot of the second, and, deciding retreat was obviously called for, threw myself into the dark caverns of the nearest shop, racing around shelves and cases to the back, where I stood panting just a little and sweating a whole lot as I peered down an aisle of dusty sandstone statues toward the entrance.

The two guys stood in the doorway, obviously looking for me. I ducked behind a big fake mummy and watched as a little bent old man in a dusty blue caftan pushed aside a bead curtain and scuffed his way out into the shop. Behind him, pausing in the bead doorway, was another guy, a dark figure in a black muscle tee, black jeans, and a long ebony braid that hung down to his shoulder blades. The two touchy-feely guys said something to the old man, but he waved his hands in a shooing motion and must have told them to get lost. They didn't like that and started coming into the shop, but the guy in black stepped forward and said something that had them hesitating. After a couple of what I was sure were snarky comments, they left.

I used the sleeve of my tee to wipe the sweat off my forehead. (Don't make that face; I didn't have anything else!) Dragging my duffel bag by its handles, I carefully made my way down the aisle toward the old man, who was waving an ancient black feather duster over some objects on a shelf in a dark corner. The guy in black was up at the front of the store, bent over looking at a case near the doorway.

I'd had enough of the guys in Egypt already, so I kept my voice low when I approached the old man.

"Ahlan wa sah." The Dig Egypt! lit said it was polite to say hello and good-bye when you entered a shop.

The old man, humming softly to himself, gave a little jump and spun around clutching the feather duster. He squinted at me and raised his hand to his face like he was going to adjust his glasses, then made a *tch* noise when he realized he wasn't wearing them.

"Salam alekum," he responded, which I knew meant "peace be with you," a polite greeting. I also knew the correct response, thanks to Mrs. Andrews.

"Wa alekum es sala. Um . . . do you speak English? *Inta bititkalim?"*

"English, yes, yes, speak English much small, much small." The old man beamed at me. *"Insha'allah,* you speak slowly."

"Whew. No problem. I'm afraid my Arabic is pretty bad, but the Dig Egypt! people say that we should pick it up quick enough once we start hanging around the workers and stuff. My name is Jan, January James. I'm going to be working on an archaeological dig in the Valley of the Servitors. The tombs out near Luxor, you know? Anyhow, I'm here for a month to work on the dig. I'm going to be a journalist, and I thought this whole Egypt thing would give me a lot of things to break into the biz with."

"Tombs, yes, yes, tombs good. Eh . . ." The old man looked confused for a moment, rubbing the sharp ridge of his nose. "Valley of Servitors?"

"Yep, that's the place." I scooted my bag next to the small table that held an ancient cash register, well away from the guy in black who was still at the front of the shop, now squatting next to a box that apparently held a bunch of tools. I looked around, figuring I might as well get my shopping for Mom and the others out of the way while I waited for the gropers outside to get tired of hanging around. "So you sell, what, antiques and stuff?" I looked into a tray of beaded necklaces next to the cash register. "Jewelry is always a good gift choice. Everyone likes jewelry."

"Yes, yes, Valley of Servitors! You come here," the little old guy said in his dusty voice, pointing to the far corner with one knobby hand while waving me toward it with the other. "You come. Valley of Servitors."

"You have some replicas of stuff from the tombs? Like statues and jewelry and things like that? I know they've found a lot of things there in the last few years. Mom would probably like something like that because it's from the area I'll be working in." I put down a pretty pink-and-red beaded necklace and followed him to the back of the room, sneezing a couple of times at the dust his caftan stirred up as he hobbled down the aisle. There was one dim bare bulb in the middle of the small shop that didn't do much to shed light in the corners, which probably did a lot to explain the old guy's squint.

"Valley of Servitors," the man repeated, stopping in front of an old black bookcase. I looked. On the shelves was a pretty motley collection of items—a small brown stone sphinx that was missing a leg, a papier-mâché King Tut's golden mask, a couple of dingy blue scarabs, three amber-and-gold beaded necklaces hanging from a rickety wooden stand, and a dirty black bracelet stuffed behind them.

I fingered the beaded necklaces, trying to see how well they'd clean up. My mother liked amber; maybe a necklace would make a good gift from Egypt? "Um . . . how much are they?" I asked, pointing to the necklaces.

"How much, yes, how much. Valley of Servitors, how much. Yes."

I sighed, almost too tired to care. My T-shirt was glued to my back despite the fact that the sun had gone down. Little rivulets of sweat snaked down the back of my neck, slid down my spine, and joined their brethren captured in the waistband of my jeans. I was sweaty, lost, and had already yelled bad things at people my first hour in this country. Rifling through my mental files labeled Things I Had to Learn Before I Got on the Plane for Egypt, I trotted out the pertinent phrase for "how much is that?" *"Bikam da?"*

"Bi-kaem?" The old guy rattled off something.

I pulled out the letter from the Dig Egypt! people that had the hotel name and address, and a pen. "Can you write it down for me? I'm not very good at numbers yet."

He wrote down the number fifty. I looked it up on the list of currency conversions Rob had printed out for me before I left home. Fifty Egyptian piastres was a little more than eight dollars—well within my souvenir-buying budget—but Mrs. Andrews had told me how much fun she had bargaining with people in the stores, and said it was expected by the shopkeepers.

I grinned at the old man and crossed out the fifty and wrote ten.

His eyes lit up as he made a clicking sound with his tongue, tipped his head back, and raised his eyebrows. "Not enough! Not enough! Valley of Servitors. You see? *Rekhis.* Very cheap." He scratched out the ten and wrote forty.

À la Andrews, I tried to look like I was so shocked by his price I'd rather staple my fingers together than pay what he asked. "Too much! Too expensive. Let's try twenty." I wrote the number down below his.

He opened his eyes really wide and slapped his hand up against the side of his face, which I assumed meant he was ready to beat himself silly before he accepted that price. His gnarled, twisted fingers grabbed my pen and wrote thirty.

I pursed my lips and looked at the necklaces, fingering the little money I had changed at the Paris airport. Thirty piastres was about five bucks. "For all of them? All three? Oh, shoot, what's three, hang on, let me look it up . . . *talat! Talat* necklaces?"

He shook his head, saying, "*Wahid, wahid,*" as he scooped up the black bracelet and plopped it down in my hand, his elderly, arthritis-riddled fingers having no difficulty in quickly extracting the thirty piastres from the money I held in my hand.

I looked down at the ugly bracelet sitting on my palm.

It was of some sort of black stone, with a small blue bird-shaped blob on the top. "Hey, wait a minute; my mother likes amber— I want the amber necklaces!"

"You take, very good. Valley of Servitors." He hobbled toward the front of the store, ignoring me as I followed slowly behind him, desperately thumbing through the Arabic phrasebook in hopes it had "I don't want this ugly bracelet, I want the three pretty amber necklaces, instead" as one of their translated phrases.

"Look . . . um . . . what's the word for old guy . . . ?"

I looked up from the phrase book just in time to avoid running into a tall black shape that said, "*Effendim.*"

"What? Oh. Thanks. *Effendim,* sir, I want the necklaces— Hey! Where'd he go?"

"In the back. Hassad is very old." The guy in black with the long hair turned to look at me. He was a little taller than me, and although he had dark hair and dark eyes like the guys outside, there was something different about him. For one, he obviously spoke English (with an accent, but it was a cool accent), and for another, he looked at me differently. The guys outside, even the older men, looked at me like I was a cherry on top of a sundae and they wanted to lick the whipped cream off, and how creepy is that? But this guy, he just looked at me like I was nothing different from any other girl. And he didn't stare at my boobs, which was a really nice change.

Until I thought about that.

Why wasn't he looking at my body? Was I that repulsive? Did he think I was too fat? Even guys who thought I was fat liked to look at my boobs, but not this guy. Oh, no, Mr. Sexy-as-sin with his long braid and his muscle tee and nummy brown eyes just looked at me like I was no more interesting than the ugly bracelet that was glued to my sweaty palm.

Sigh. Some days life just wasn't worth the trouble of chewing through the leather straps on the straitjacket.

The Year My Life Went Down the Loo
by Katie Maxwell

Subject: The Grotty and the Fabu (No, it's not a song.)
From: Mrs.Oded@btelecom.co.uk
To: Dru@seattlegrrl.com

Things That Really Irk My Pickle About Living in England

- The school uniform
- Piddlington-on-the-weld (I will forever be known as Emily from *Piddlesville*)
- Marmite (It's yeast sludge! GACK!)
- The ghost in my underwear drawer (Spectral hands fondling my bras—enough said!)
- No malls! What are these people *thinking???*

Things That Keep Me From Flying Home to Seattle for Good Coffee

- Aidan (*Hunkalicious!*)
- Devon (*Droolworthy?* Understatement of the year!*)
- Fang (He puts the *num* in *nummy!*)
- Holly (Any girl who hunts movie stars with me—and Oded Fehr *will be mine*—is a friend for life.)
- Über-coolio Polo Club (Where the snogging is FINE!)

Didn't want this book to end?

There's more waiting at **www.smoochya.com**:

Win FREE books and makeup!
Read excerpts from other books!
Chat with the authors!
Horoscopes!
Quizzes!

 smooch Bringing you the books on everyone's lips!